Deadly Magnolia

A Novel

By Arielle L. Crowell

Literati Media Group

characters who suffer them, were created within the dark realm of my own imagination (however demented it may be). Thank you!

Cover art provided by: Lauren M. Biggs of Literati Media Group. For information on graphic design work, please contact Lauren at literatimediagroup@gmail.com

Also, for information on Author Arielle Crowell, please visit her author website at http://www.ariellecrowell.com.

For more information on the publisher, please visit the website at: http://www.literatimediagroup.com

Note from the Author

(disclaimer)

To my magnificent readers who adore indulging on the mysterious, the dramatic, and the scandalous, I wanted to impress upon you the nature of this book and some of the seemingly "sick" events that take place within it. The events which are to come are purely a means to convey the sanity or lack thereof of my character. Anyone who is not of sound mind may very well take interactions with others to a very demented and unstable place- especially without the proper treatment.

My character's crimes are extremely violent, unpredictable, and particularly heinous in the eyes of a sane person. And I feel it's important that you know that I find his crimes and habits just as disgusting and horrible as you, but I still felt compelled to give him to all of you. I certainly don't want him sitting around in my head somewhere collecting dust, giving me nightmares.

At any rate, I just wanted to let you know that I realize he is extremely deranged, just as I realize that the persons who abused him were just as heinous as he is. When you read this book, please keep this in mind. The individual is sick, and it is meant to be conveyed just that way. Likewise the character's priest and mother are particularly despicable as well. I realize this, but the story had to be told.

I would also like to ask that you don't take this book too seriously. Yes, belief, as with any fictional book to some degree, must be suspended just a little. Let's hope that people aren't really this crazy. And if they are, run like hell. But do keep in mind that this book and all its contents are strictly for entertainment purposes only.

In addition I would like to express that I am in no way, shape, or form a practitioner of voodoo. I just find the subject particularly fascinating and like writing about it. The symbol that you see throughout the book is a voodoo veve for Erzulie who is akin to The Virgin Mary in Christianity.

With that, please enjoy!

Thank you

-Arielle

Acknowledgments

First and foremost, I must always thank God. Without God, nothing would be possible- not life, not talent, not happiness, nor love… nothing. So you see, in my mind, first thanks must always go to Him because it all starts with Him. He is the beginning and the end, and has given me all that I have. For that, I am thankful.

Secondly, I think it incredibly imperative that I give thanks to my parents, Lee and Hillary Crowell. I can not say that we agree on everything… never have and probably never will, but that doesn't negate the fact that my parents are probably some of the greatest parents a person can have. They are supportive, firm in their convictions, but willing to listen when it counts. They have helped me through a lot of transitional tough times in my life and I honestly can't say where I'd be without them. They've always tried to do the best they could by me and all my siblings. I am blessed to have them. So in case I haven't said it enough or shown it enough, please know that I thank you both whole heartedly. I really do appreciate everything that you have done and continue to do for me and my son.

Thirdly, I must thank my spectacular team at Literati Media Group who have worked so hard with me to make these projects become a reality. Adenike Lucas, Lauren Biggs, Kenneth Smith, and Bruce Lucas have all played pivotal parts to making our dream of owning our own publishing house and presenting our work to the public real and tangible. Trying to stay motivated is hard work, let me tell you, but you fabulous four could inspire a dead person to do the dougie. ☺

A special thank you to Lauren, especially, for the fabulous book cover that brought life to my book as well as the sisterly bond we have developed over the past 12-13 years. And to Bruce for working so diligently and without complaint on my book trailer. I really appreciate your efforts and the way you just jump right in and get things done even when I'm (eternally) procrastinating.

And to my good friend, Steve Beasley, who was very supportive in filming the book trailer as the lead role, thank you so much! I really appreciate how you weren't afraid to do anything we asked. Your participation was a great addition to my project and I hope you'll agree to be a part of many more projects in the future. Your energy is amazing!

To my son, Kingston, once again you're always an inspiration. I can still hear your little five year old voice asking me "Mommy, what are you doing? Are you writing books on your computer so we can have a place to live?" Haha, and though we weren't quite in a state where we had no place to live, it always made me laugh that you knew, to some degree, that I was writing these books to make our lives better. So I guess for your part, thank you for understanding.

To my best-friends, Carmen Grandison, Alicia Nichols Dash, Denise Brown, Syreeta Hill, Lauren Biggs (again) and Dianne Long Morris: I love each and every one of you. All of you, in your own ways, have been super supportive of everything that I have done, even when I was acting crazy as hell (which I'm still pretty prone to do). And though we are all scattered across the east coast, love has never been lost between us, and you can not know just how important that is to me. We have more than a friendship. It is a sisterhood. I am eternally thankful to have had all of you in my life for the past 15 years. Now, soak up this mushy moment because I'm pretty sure you won't be getting another from me this lifetime! ☺

I must give thanks to my brother, David Benjamin Crowell, my brother Lee Crowell III, my excellent friend, Dwight Ridley, as well as my male bff, Eric Littlejohn. You guys have given me great support and always encouraged me to continue writing. Dwight, I find that the deep philosophical conversations that you and I always seem to have help to give my characters depth and human flaws. I doubt you knew you had such impact on what I write but you absolutely do, and I always value the time we spend talking. Eric, thank you for always being there even when I clearly pluck your nerves and act like a spoiled little brat. It's my nature, and I love that you can accept this about me and still hang tough.

To my sissy poo, Joi Fontaine, thank you for allowing me to crash at your house all the times you did when I was running up and down the road for Literati Media Group business. You're a typical big sister, pushing me around, but you've always been supportive in your own special way. I appreciate all the love.

To my good friend, Brandon "Boogie B" Montrell, all the way in LA: I really appreciate you telling me how wonderful and special you think I am. I was humbled by you telling me that I should never settle and never allow anyone to treat me less than what I am- a good person and a Queen. Thank you for that because sometimes I tend to forget and beat myself up too much. I read the letter you sent me sometimes and become inspired all over again. Your words had a helluva impact on my drive.

To Mistah (Travis) – and yes we will just leave it at Mistah, thank you for putting up with us trampling through the house and eating all the food for those Literati meetings. I'm sure you were tired of looking at us but we thank you for your patience anyway ☺.

To Sabrina Smith-Dalrymple, thank you for editing the content of Deadly Magnolia, and providing me with excellent suggestions on making the book better. I really appreciated all that you did to help me!

To Mr. Anthony Biggs, thank you so much for modeling for the cover. Without your help and participation, my cover would not have been as special as it was. You brought life and a face to the book, and for that I am forever grateful.

Last but most definitely not least, to my readers, I appreciate that you have once again taken a chance on me and my incredibly eccentric imagination in order to read this book. I'm always humbled and so overjoyed that you continue to take the time to voyage with me on such a crazy journey into the unknown, daring to read what is sure to be something absolutely insane. Thank you always and eternally for your support. Without you all, I don't think much of this would have come to pass. And though I may never see you or speak with you personally- though you may be miles and miles away from where I am and our paths may never physically cross, I want you all to know that from the bottom of my heart, I love you. Each and every one of you... more than words will allow me to express.

Thank you all!

Most lovingly,

-Ari

Deadly Magnolia

A Novel

By Arielle L. Crowell

Nicodemus, the slave, was of African birth

And was bought for a bagful of gold

He was reckoned as part of the salt of the earth

But he died years ago very old…

Nicodemus was a prophet, at least was as wise

For he told of battles to come

And we trembled with dread as he rolled up his eyes

And we heeded the shake of his thumb…

-"Wake Nicodemus" by Henry Clay, 1864

PROLOGUE

Covered in blood that wasn't his own, Nicodemus banged his battered hands desperately at the door of the beaten down shack on the corner of Dauphine and Orleans Street. It was the same shack that no one in their right mind would ever visit thanks to the decrepit ole witch with the white eyes who lived there. Not only was there a witch living there, but the house itself was cloaked in darkness and a debilitating cold. Even on the warmest and brightest of days, that place was chilly, concealed in shadows, and smelled like rotten meat.

He ran there, panicked and paranoid, during the middle of one of the deadliest storms New Orleans had ever seen. It wasn't quite Katrina, but it was damn close. There was no doubt in his mind that whatever was hunting him had caused the horrible storm that was abusing the city like it was- slamming the streets with torrential downpours, deafening thunder, and blinding lightning. *It* wanted to stop him. *It* wanted him dead… maybe even worse. *It*… the Evil… *her* Evil. *It* wanted to devour him.

He ran there as fast as his blood spattered legs and feet would carry him, desperate to get there before a demonic apparition- *l'envoi morts,*[1] had the chance to snuff out his life… Or before the police caught up with him for all the murders, whichever came first. Both entities would mean an ass load of trouble either way you sliced it, but he preferred the cops. It was better to be locked in jail forever than to be left at the mercy of The Evil or whatever it was coming for him.

Damn it! Why had he done the things he'd done? Where was his self-control? Hadn't his *granmére*[2] taught him that there are consequences for everything that you do? *Mess with another person's life and the spirits will even the score… that is the balance of things, Nicodemus.* That's what he could hear her voice saying to him in that incessant warning tone that she would always use, as she sat rubbing a bit of salve on her swollen ankles after his mother had beaten him black blue for whatever horrific thing he'd done. But now… now it was too late. Now *it* was going to rip his soul to shreds. That's what *it* wanted after all- his soul.

Time was running out… slipping away from him like sand in an hour glass. If he didn't hurry, *it* would

---

[1] *L'envoi morts*- the sending of a death spirit after a person
[2] *Granmére*- grandmother

catch up to him; and his body would be deader than a rusty, old, door nail.

Holding his achy sides with bloody hands, he had sloshed down the street, muddying his clothes, with water squishing in his expensive leather shoes while looking for her quarters. There, he hoped to finally find peace... or at least a safe haven from the storm before the flood whisked him away to a watery death. Who knows how long those levees would hold before the city was buried beneath treacherous waters? But then again, even drowning would be better than what was in store for him.

Lucien had known what he was up against... or at least he said he knew. But where was he now? Why hadn't he come with him down there? It was just like him to leave! *Damn him for always leaving*! Still, Lucien had at least tried to help him... he had to give him that. He had been the one to suggest that Nico find the old witch in the first place. Lucien had said everyone knew who she was... that she was notorious on the voodoo scene for helping people in need and Nico certainly was a man in need at that point.

He told Nico that he could find her down in the darkest corners of the French Quarter, where the spirit world met the living one. He'd said he'd know he'd come to the right place when he could smell death in the air. Not festering, dead bodies not yet buried, but old, ancient death that had lain still in wormy earth for centuries waiting for the chance to walk the streets again. This was the death that consumed the air around the old shack, choking the life out of anyone stupid enough to knock on the door. And he was...

As the lightning ripped open the sky, and the rain bled from the wound, Nico could see the creeping shadows closing in on him- shadows with claws, horns, and hooves. Shadows of demons- *djabs*,[3] who had come for the damned.

"*Bondye mwen*[4]! Lady, open this damn door," he exclaimed as he banged his bloodied fists on the tattered door again, anxious to get inside. "They're going to kill me! Hurry up!"

The lightning cracked again, and he could suddenly see *her* face in the flash... *her* angry, vengeful face. He blinked frantically, trying to get the image that stalked him daily out of his mind. Everywhere he turned, she was there... she and that damn Magnolia blossom. He cursed the day he'd ever laid eyes on that white flower. It did nothing but bring him misery.

He gasped, looking around feeling his heart thundering in his chest. What was *she* going to do to him? He knew it was *she* who had sent spirits... *She* who was the cause of the Evil... And if he became a slave, it would be *she* who would be his master... his oppressor.

"Oh God," he whimpered. "Please..."

---

[3] *Djab*- devil; wild, wicked, aggressive spirit
[4] *Bondye Mwen*- Creole (Kreyol) for "My God"

"*Ki moun ki la*[5]?" he heard an old, raspy voice hiss harshly. "Oo' be dere?"

The door creaked open slowly, groaning painfully on its rusted, ancient hinges. The old, wrinkled crone with blanched, white eyes- eyes that seemed to sear right through Nico and burn into his soul stood there "*staring*" at him. He shuddered as she pointed her crooked, skeletal finger with sagging skin and long, yellowed nail, at him.

"Ah, 'tis you. Yeh come 'ere t'do de Devil's work, Nicodemus LaCroix or yeh come 'ere t'save yer damned soul? Eit'er way, dere be a bad man at me door."

Her voice was raspy and worn... like an old record that had been playing over and over buried beneath graveyard dust.

"M- *Madame* Sepion? Uh... I... uh... Wait a minute. How do you know my name? You- you... know me?"

The old woman, whose face was cracked and wizened like crumpled paper, shuffled aside and motioned for Nico to enter.

"*Entre*[6]."

He pushed past the old woman, nearly knocking her down, thrilled to finally be safe.

---

[5] *Ki moun ki la*- Creole (Kreyol) for "who is there?"
[6] *Entre*- Come in (Creole/Kreyol)

Inside, the little shack was rundown and timeworn; probably built in the early 1800's or maybe even before. *Madame* Sepion lit an ancient oil lamp which still used whale oil. It offered more of an eerie, supernatural glow than actual light. Nico could see the dark demonic shadows dancing across her yellowed, peeling walls in the glow of the ghostly lamp. He took a deep breath.

"I was told that you could help me," Nico said feeling frightened. "How did you know it was me? Did Lucien call and tell you I was coming? Wait- do you even have a phone? I mean Lucien told me to come here, so he must have told you I was coming right?"

The old woman chortled, chuckling and snorting at the same time.

"I doan know nobody name dat, but I know oo' yeh be, Nicodemus LaCroix. Yeh be de last livin' descendant o'Nicodemus Christophe LaCroix, come 'ere in de days o' de migration from Saint Domingue[7]. All o' Nawlins respect 'im den, dis man dat come 'ere wit' great 'onor. But 'im great-great grandson… tsk tsk tsk… I 'ear 'e be a coward. I 'ear 'e be a man dat must suffer *Lanmó*[8] many times over. *Tant pis.*"[9]

Nico's breath caught in his throat making him cough like he was hacking up a lung. The woman,

---

[7] Saint Domingue- Haiti
[8] *Lanmó*- Creole (Kreyol) word for Death
[9] *Tant pis*- too bad

hunched over like an old, rotted tree, was as blind as a bat, but she could see straight through him.

"I- I...," he stumbled trying to regain his composure. "I don't know what you've heard about me, but maybe you've heard that I'm running for Senator. I'm a great politician! I'm going to be Senator of Lousiana in the near future, but I've got some problems that I have to take care of first. I need your help. I was told to see *Madame* Sepion- that I could find help here- that you're a *mambo*.[10] Is that true? Do you know the magic that can help me get my life back and make things normal again? Please say you'll help me."

The old woman let a ghoulish smile cross her thin, cracked lips as she sat down on a wooden chair, which groaned in pain from her weight.

"I doan know 'bou' dat. De spirits tell me 'bou' you but dey doan say no'ting bou' no Sen'tor. No- dey say yeh corrupt de souls o' ot'ers. Yeh be a bad man, *Mesieur*[11] LaCroix. Not like yer ancestor 'fore yeh. Yer soul will rot in de jar o' de *bokor*[12] an' you will die a slave. I come 'ere from Haiti t'get 'way from de black magic dere. I doan' need dose pwoblems 'ere. Now tyake yer bad blood an' leave dis place."

"No, I can't! Don't send me back out there! I just told you it's crazy as shitfire out there! Didn't I just tell

---

[10] *Mambo-* vodou priestess
[11] *Mesieur-* Creole (Kreyol) word for Mr.
[12] *Bokor-* powerful master of voodoo magic who uses black magic

you the bastards are trying to kill me?! I need back up for all this shit!"

"*Ki sa ou vle, Mesieur* La Croix?[13] Why do yeh bot'er an ole woman?"

Nico swallowed, feeling his heart about to beat right out of his chest.

"There's something coming for me… trying to- to turn me into- Don't you see? I'm going crazy! And I'm *not* crazy, okay? I'm *not*! No matter what Lucien says! But, all the old legends are true! I didn't even believe it myself before now, but I swear… I- I… *it* makes me do things… *She* makes me!"

"Humph! Nobody myake yeh do no'ting! Yeh jus' evil! An' de *lwa*[14] comin' t' drag yeh t' hell, *Mesieur*. Dey wan' yer soul t' burn in dis life an' de nex'. Wan' yeh t' suffer. *Lwa* doan bring no curse t' ot'ers, but dey let dis curse come fer yeh. Dey let de bokor's demons come. Jus' lis'en!"

Lightning stabbed the sky so fiercely that Nico swore it had torn some ancient tree into splinters. The thunder snarled so loudly it threatened to shake the little shack to bits. The wind whooped and whined, swaying the little house as if it meant to bring it to its knees. *It* was there to kill him, he could tell, and *it* was growing impatient. He looked warily at the door as the shadows in

---

[13] *Ki sa ou vle*- Creole (Kreyol) for "what do you want?"
[14] *Lwa*- spirits in the pantheon of Vodou

the room seemed to loom over him like hungry predators ready to pounce. Should he run?

"Can yeh 'ear dem? Dey speak t' me, *Mesieur*. Dey say yer flesh will rot wit' de maggots and yer soul will walk de eart' as a zombie! Oh yes, 'tis so. Not'ing I can do. Yer soul be damned."

Nico swallowed, unable to accept what he was hearing. He was Nicodemus LaCroix damn it- the future Senator of Louisiana! There was no way in hell anybody was going to do a damn thing to his soul! Not without a fight first!

He frantically dug down deep into his pocket with his bloody fingers trembling, and pulled out wads of clammy cash soaked from the rain. He pushed it in the blind woman's hand desperately.

"Here, lady! That's 500 fuckin' dollars and there's plenty more where that came from! Help me! I need you to save my life before-"

"Yer life? Hahahahahahaha, "she cackled. "Yer life means no'ting t' me, *Mesieur*, no'ting! Yer life be gone already if me had it me way! Me doan 'elp no wort'less man. A dead man! An' look a' yeh... t'ink yeh can bribe de spirits, eh? Tsk tsk tsk. *Enbesil*[15]," the old woman interrupted.

---

[15] *Enbesil*- Dummy in Creole (Kreyol)

"Look, I'm rich, okay? I don't give a damn about spirits or any of that old mumbo jumbo! I will run this entire state once I'm elected to office and none of that shit will matter! But right now, you gotta believe me! Something is trying to kill me! Do you understand? Something is trying to take my sanity away from me! I'm doing things… I'm-I… my wife… she's…"

Madame Sepion stared at him without staring at him at all, but he could feel her milky white eyes undressing him. She tucked the soaking wet money into the folds of her dress and pulled out a handful of old, yellowed bones. She shook them in her ancient hands and spread them out on a wooden table next to her chair.

"Dere's a curse on yer soul, *Mesieur* LaCroix… a mos' deserved curse. Bones say it be someone yeh 'ave wronged. An' she sen' an Evil fer you. *L'envoi morts*! Bones say deat' spirit will tyake yer mind… will tyake yer *ti bon ange*[16]… an' enslave you 'fore yeh die. Make yeh de living dead. It be an old punishmen' from de ole days in Haiti. Work o' de *San Pwel*[17]… de secret societies some say, but I doan know no *San Pwel* 'ere in dis country.

"Whoever it be, de *Lwa* will not 'elp yeh. Dey doan care if yeh die. Bones say, dat you bring a scourge 'pon de 'oliness o' marriage. Yeh done stirred

---

[16] *Ti bon ange*- part of the soul that houses the personality, conscience, and free thinking

[17] San Pwel- Creole for without skin- members of the Haitian secret societies (Bizango)

Damballah's[18]wrath 'cause yeh treat yer wife bad. Now, yeh tell me, *Mesieur* LaCroix, whuh yeh done t' deserve such punishmen'? Hmm? Whuh yeh done t' 'ave yer *ti bon ange* tyaken 'way?"

"What the hell? I don't even know what that is!"

"Doan worry, *Mesieur.* Yeh goan' fine' out soon enuff. Not goan' be pretty eit'er. Now whuh yeh do? Me know yeh do somet'ing. Me know yeh deserve t' die. Tell me now."

Nico sighed.

"I... my wife... my first wife, you see... I'm... It was The Bad Thing! It made me- The singing- Look, it doesn't matter what I've done. I just need you to shake up your cat bones or whatever it is you do to get these fucks off my back! I know I'm not crazy, but they wanna make me think I am, see? They think if I go crazy that I won't run for Senate. You see? See the plan? They think they can stop me! But I've got the majority vote! Now listen to me, I paid you money for your help. Now help me! Enough with these questions! You're really starting to piss me off and trust me, you don't want it with me!"

Madame Sepion cackled like an old witch as spit flew from her shriveled mouth. Her eyes were as blank as paper but seemed bright and alive with amusement at Nico's fate.

---

[18] *Damballah-* Voudou lwa; the serpernt; protector of the handicapped, crippled, deformed, albinos, and young children

"I doan' tyake no orders from you, *kochon*[19]! Yeh be a dead man by sunrise wit' out me 'elp! You will do whuh *I* say! Do yeh 'ear me, or-yeh- *die*!"

She dug into the folds of her dress again, the same folds she'd tucked away Nico's money. She pulled out a leathery, molded, shrunken head that had white maggots eating away at the grey skin and sewn up eyes. She dangled it in Nico's face by its coarse, black hair.

"*Bondye mwen*! You're fuckin' crazy! What the fuck is that?"

"Yeh wan' dis t' be you? *Djab la manje moun nan*[20] . Dey will do de same t'yeh! Kill yeh! *Eat* yeh! Yeh doan' 'ave much time. Me 'ear dem gettin' closer an' closer. Den yer body be a slave forever! An' when yeh finally die, yeh be jus' like 'im," she said plucking the shrunken head with her long nail. "Yeh wan' me t' 'elp stop dis, *Mesieur* LaCroix, yeh tell me whuh yeh done t' be cursed. Ot'erwise, get out me house."

Nico looked at the door and saw the face of a black demon covered in shadows. His eyes grew wide with fear.

"If I tell you, will you help me" he exclaimed frantically.

---

[19] *Kochon*- Creole (Kreyol) for "pig," as in a disgusting man
[20] *Djab la manje moun nan*- Creole (Kreyol) for "the djab ate the person" which means the spirit consumed the person's life force or gros (gwo) bon ange

Madame Sepion's white eyes narrowed and her cracked smile widened in that eerie light.

"*Si Bondye vle²¹*."

"Okay! Okay, fine! I'll tell you! But you have to promise not to tell Lucien! He'll be so angry! He's already pissed at me!"

---

²¹ *Si Bondye vle*- Creole (Kreyol) for "If God wants"

CHAPTER I

"How much longer do we have to wait, baby? You know my manager has got me booked for a couple shows on the west coast and I wanna hit up Rodeo Drive while I'm out there. I need you to break me off with some of that dough."

"Lee, I really can't right now," Nico said calmly. "Now is not the proper time to-"

"What the fuck do you mean, you can't? You know what? You really need to hurry this shit up. Got me waiting forever for this money and a husband like I'm some desperate ass side hoe... You got me fucked up! You shoulda been got rid of that bitch. We were supposed to have been married by now. But nah, you still playing house with her stuck up ass and got me waiting. I'ma tell you what, though. I ain't the one!"

Nico sighed, wishing that she'd just shut the hell up all together. Her voice reminded him of his mother's- grating, nerve wrecking, and nagging. On and on and on,

Aleera talked about the same thing every day. When was enough going to be enough? She was a mistress for God's sake, not his wife. She needed to play the mistress position and shut the fuck up about everything else. Her job was to pleasure him sexually, not to nag him. He had a wife for that.

He had made it perfectly clear from the beginning that he was already married to someone else, but she didn't give a damn about that. She still insisted that he marry her. It was starting to really piss him off and she certainly didn't want to do that if she knew what was good for her. She had no idea what he was capable of, but she was damn sure going to find out. If she wasn't careful he would gift her two black eyes to wear to those west coast shows that she was so excited about… maybe a broken nose and jaw to match. Girls like to coordinate don't they?

Besides, it's not like he hadn't told her that he wasn't getting a divorce... ever. Hell, he'd married a beautiful woman from a prestigious Southern Black Family- the Blanchards. There wasn't a person in the New Orleans area that didn't know their name.

His wife, the coveted beauty, Marielle Blanchard, had inherited the family plantation estate, along with a helluva fortune stemming back to the 1800s. The family was descended from the mulatto elite-*gens de couleur*[22]

---

[22] *Gens de couleur*- "people of color" name given to the governing elite in Haiti after the slave revolt and departure of the French in the 1800s

who had come to the US from Haiti spreading the sugar cane trade. That meant he was rolling around in old money, doing what he wanted when he wanted with one of the most beautiful women in the state. And to think he'd bagged Marielle after a twenty year stint in a mental institution. What more could a guy ask for?

He didn't know what gave Aleera the impression that he was leaving all of that behind just to be with her. He wasn't going anywhere, and it'd be in her best interest to stop asking him about it before that mental illness he'd been hiding so well flared his temper.

Still, he didn't want to come off like an asshole... at least not right now while his wife was lurking somewhere in the house. The last thing he needed was for her to hear him arguing on the phone with his mistress. She'd go nuclear. Then in retaliation she'd cook one of those pies that always made him feel funny and made him black out. Or maybe she'd cut the head off a chicken and put the blood in a pot of spaghetti for him to eat. Then he'd have a few weird dreams about people in black robes with white ash all over their faces dragging him through a black cemetery. It would scare the hell out of him and he'd be too afraid to say a word to Marielle for weeks. And she would smile knowingly like she knew what was happening inside his head at night. His wife knew way too much about conjuring roots and he damn sure didn't need her messing around with him like that all over Aleera.

Besides all that, if he did come off like an ass, Aleera would probably stop giving him all that wild, freak nasty pussy she always gave him and he'd be forced to take it from her instead. Taking pussy was always a messy business and he certainly didn't have time to listen to all that screaming. He sighed.

"Lee," he said slowly, as if he were talking to a child, carefully choosing his words. "I don't want to talk about this anymore, okay? I'm tired and I have a meeting with my campaign manager tomorrow. I have several speeches that I need to prepare and the last thing on my mind is marrying my mistress. As for money, you know I can't wire you any right now. My wife will see whatever I take out of our account and she will question me about it. And how do you think I would explain that? She's not stupid you know; and this is technically *her* money."

Aleera sucked her teeth.

"I'm so fuckin' tired of the bullshit, Nico! You know that? I'm tired of all your lame ass excuses! Everyday it's something new! I've been with your moody ass for two years. You think I'm gonna wait on you forever like I don't have shit else to do? Hell nah, nigga! You got the wrong one!"

Nico sighed feeling his temper slowly slip away, but somehow, he'd have to control it. After all, his mentor, Dr. Thibideaux, always told him *progression not regression*. He'd worked hard to maintain some form of tranquility all these years. He certainly didn't want to lose all that progress now on account of Aleera. He took a deep breath.

"Look, I don't know what the problem is. I care about you, but that's about as far as it goes. You know I can't leave my wife. I've got my career to think about. I'm not jeopardizing that, so you may as well cut the dramatics. You're starting to grate on my last nerve."

"Well, what about me? Oh so I ain't as important as your career or your little prim and proper wife? I guess I ain't shit, huh? I'm just the chick you come to when you want a nut!"

Nico could feel the vein in each of his temples start to throb and ache… a clear sign that things could get ugly. In the two years they'd been having their little affair, Nico had never put his hands on her in a violent way. Oh sure they had rough sex here and there, but nothing too serious. He had always been able to calm himself down before things went too far with her. Still, she had no idea what kind of violent thoughts lurked in his cloudy mind. But the more she nagged him, the closer she was to finding out just who he really was. Each day he fought the urge to grab her by her horse hair and force her mouth shut by shoving a fist into it.

"Listen, I'm taking a chance even continuing to mess around with you. Don't you understand that a divorce would seriously damage my career? My wife will divorce my ass if I ever get caught with you. So really, I'm doing you a favor even still fuckin' you, Lee. You're a beautiful girl, don't get me wrong. You have a very sexy body. But marry you? Ha! Ain't gonna happen, *chére*[23]. And please don't act brand new like this is news to you. Let's just enjoy the ride while it lasts, hear?"

"What? Are you kidding me? You know what, Nico? You're a piece of shit! I don't know why I've let you fuck me and leave me like this for the past two years. If your wife was so fuckin' great, why are you always over here trying to get some of my pussy? Huh? Answer me that! 'Cause that Creole twat ain't like ghetto twat, bruh! That's why!"

Nico's hands balled into a fist and he felt that familiar burning sensation behind his eyes… the one that always ended with him in a blind rage. A woman should respect a man, not talk shit to him. The way Aleera spoke to him with all that hostility and attitude made him want to put her head through a wall. All he could see was red clouding his eyes with hazy, hot anger. Visions of her bloody, mutilated body flashed quickly in his mind changing his physical and mental demeanor entirely. All his niceties faded to black and all that was left was bitter, black, bile.

"Let me tell you something, bitch," he spat bitterly. "That's the last time you ever come out of your fuckin' mouth like that to me! Do you hear me? The next time you talk to me like that, I will bash your fuckin' brains in

---

[23] *Chére*- dear, sweetie

and feed that slop to my dogs! Do you fuckin' understand me, you cunt!"

Aleera took the phone away from her ear and stared stupidly at it. She'd never heard Nico say anything so mean and raw before. He was always trying to talk like he was some kind of high class aristocrat. Now he was acting straight gully. She wasn't even sure she was talking to the same person.

"I could never marry somebody like you with your filthy ass mouth," he continued. "You think the future Senator of Louisiana could be seen with a ghetto ass gutter rat like you? Fuck no, you dirty bitch! A Senator's wife should be a refined woman who understands Southern Traditions! You're nothing but a broken down, country cunt who-"

Before Nico could finish his sentence, the sensual scent of lemon, vanilla, and creamy honeysuckle drifted into the room, filling the air with the signature smell of Magnolias. Nico knew immediately that Marielle had rounded the corner and entered the parlour behind him. She always wore a white Magnolia blossom in her long black hair. He could smell it in her hair even if he didn't see her. Experience had taught his nose to know that particular scent anywhere he smelled it.

"Look, I'll speak to you about this at a later time. I've got more important matters that I need to attend to."

"Nico, baby, I'm sorry... just wait. Don't hang up. I'm so-"

Nicodemus hit END on his iPhone, deading the conversation between himself and his mistress.

Marielle stood looking at him hatefully, knowing damn well he'd been talking to *that woman*. She'd known for some time now that he'd been sleeping with the ratchet, ghetto R&B singer who seemed to think *she* was Mrs. Nicodemus LaCroix.

Marielle rolled her eyes. As if anyone really would want to be married to Nico. Hell, she didn't even want him. She was just stuck with him. She had said those marriage vows before God thinking she could take a handsome man like him and make him suitable for society, but that didn't mean that she liked his trifling ass.

He wasn't the type of husband who was loyal, loving, and cherished his wife. No, he was a liar, a cheater, and a crazy lunatic most of the time. There used to be a time when he'd come home with a fresh bouquet of her favorite flowers or he'd write her a beautiful poem just to make her smile, but those days seemed to fade away into the faint whispers of southern breezes ages ago. Now she was stuck with the fascade of a loving man who really only sought to cover up the monster within who lurked right beneath the surface.

In her opinion, Nico was psychotic. His temper reminded her of Jack Nicholson's in *The Shining*- volatile.

There were too many times when she had been forced to pay for repairs in the house where Nico had punched a hole clean through the wall or kicked through a door when he'd had his sudden fits of rage over stupid things. Bathwater too hot or *café au lait*[24] not hot enough… Anything could set him off… even The Young & The Restless.

He'd even gone so far as to batter some of the servants. One time, he even beat their personal chef, Alexandre, into a coma for putting too many onions in the *vichyssoise*[25]. Marielle had been forced to pay off the man's medical expenses. She gave a hefty 5 million dollar pay off to his family in exchange for silence. She certainly didn't want a scandal attached to her family's good name.

The Blanchards were a highly respected family in New Orleans high society and anything dramatic or improper was frowned upon. There was no way in hell that she'd ever let Nico's temper destroy what they'd worked so hard to build. She may have been foolish enough to love him despite his mental problems thinking that he would love her too, but now that she knew the truth, she wouldn't allow him be the one to bring shame to her family. She had to hide his craziness from everyone and had been doing so for ten years.

---

[24] *Café au lait*- coffee with milk
[25] *Vichyssoise*- thick soup made of pureed leaks, onions, potatoes, cream, and chicken stock

She was able to control him with a bit of her *granmére's* root-work. Maybe a spell here or there, or a bit of *belladonna*[26] in his tea to keep him calm and slightly sedated... But how long could she expect to live like that, drugging her husband or casting voodoo spells on him to keep him from being his true self?

Nico, unaware of his wife's thoughts, turned to look at her and smiled charmingly, exposing his perfect, pearly white teeth and deep dimples in each cheek. He had a sexy, charismatic smile that could make a woman melt. Marielle almost had doubts even now if she should go through with what she had planned just looking at that smile.

There was no doubt that she had the finest man out there with his smooth, brown skin and neatly trimmed goatee, looking like a sophisticated Lance Gross. At 42, he didn't look a day over 30. He was in tip top shape with the physique of a young athlete, standing over 6'2" tall with muscles. So sad that such a fine specimen of a man was such a horror to be with... He was a man that every woman wanted and envied her for having, but at what cost would Marielle keep him?

"Ah, chérie mwen[27], I didn't hear you come in. Tell me, how was your day at the spa," he asked lovingly.

"I wasn't at the spa, Nico," she replied dryly.

---

[26] *Belladonna*- another name for Deadly Nightshade, a plant that can be used to relax or sedate but is deadly in excessive doses
[27] *Cherie mwen*- Creole (Kreyol) for my dear

"Really? How odd considering Pierre informed me that you'd gone to the spa today. I will have to speak to him about that. Well then, why don't *you* tell me where you were today? And Marielle, if you were with another man, I don't think I have to tell you how this is going to end."

He said it sweetly, but his voice was dripping with hidden poison. The man he'd hired to follow Marielle, Pierre Montrell, spent all his time reporting her whereabouts to Nico in fifteen minute intervals. This way he was always aware of everything his wife did.

"If you must know, I went to see Ari Goldstein- my family lawyer. I paid Pierre $500 to keep his mouth shut about it so quite obviously, he wouldn't have reported my whereabouts to you today."

Nico felt his face flush and his body temperature began to change. That numbing feeling that sometimes came in his fingertips began to make his hands tingle.

"And what were you doing with a lawyer, Marielle? Acquiring new property, perhaps? Or is there some pressing legal matter to which we need to attend?"

Marielle cleared her throat wanting to get it over with. There would be hell to pay, but there was no sense prolonging it.

"Yes, Nicodemus, I would say that there *is* a pressing legal matter that needs to be resolved. I've had divorce papers drawn up. I've decided that the time has come to end this marriage. This charade has gone on long enough."

Nico felt his eyes suddenly darken. The pupils would always seem to dilate when he got angry, almost making them completely black. He could feel his left eye twitch rapidly and his stomach clenched tight like a fist.

"What did you just say, Mari? I don't think I heard you correctly. For a minute I thought you said you wanted a divorce, but I know that can't be right."

Marielle took a step away from him and a deep breath. It was now or never. She needed to get the hell away from his ass before he took things too far. The last thing she needed was another hole in the wall or another lawsuit to dodge. Or worse: a bloody nose or broken jaw that he'd come damn close to giving her on a few occasions. Like the time she'd hugged her cousin Francois just a second too long at the Christmas Party… Hell had come to Earth that night, and it had cost her $20,000 worth of repair work in the house fixing holes in the walls.

Marielle cleared her throat. She wanted to be clear.

"I said I'm done with this marriage, Nicodemus. I've given it ten long years and I've gotten nothing out of it. No kids… no love… no companionship… nothing. All you've ever done is treat me like I'm premium real estate that you acquired through a business deal. You don't treat me like a wife, and you certainly don't respect me as one.

It's time you and I move on with our lives *separately* because you were never interested in making a life *together.*"

She said the words bitterly, allowing some of the pain that her heart felt to creep into her voice. She wanted to sound strong and stable, but her voice cracked. She had actually really loved Nico. That's why, despite his insanity, she'd never allowed her family to bring harm to him even though they were more than capable of doing so. Nico would have been a dead man long ago if it hadn't been for the love Marielle had for him.

Nico stood there stunned as each word hit his chest like a ton of bricks. He could feel the pressure mounting in his head, causing his blood pressure to rise. His head was throbbing like a heartbeat and he could hear it pounding in his ears like the beat of a drum. His chest tightened and his vision blurred. He was going to blow soon.

Gotdamn her, he thought to himself as he gritted his teeth, listening to them scrape against each other as he added more and more pressure. *Gotdamn her all to hell!*

He stared at her, only seeing a blurry figure drenched in red as the pressure in his head finally exploded to his ears, pumping hot adrenaline through his body. In an instant, he seized her arm, wringing her roughly towards him with a growl. The whites of his eyes were beginning to turn red, and his perfect, pearly whites were bared like a rabid pit bull.

"You listen to me, Marielle! We *are* each other's lives! You hear me? There's no changing that! You're never going to change that! Do you know what I'll do to you? Huh? Do you know what I'll do if you try to leave me?! Do you? Answer me, gotdamn it!"

"Let me go," Marielle said softly, almost whimpering, feeling the pressure from his fingers digging into her arm.

Nicodemus trembled as he held her arm. *What to do? Let her go or bash her fuckin' brains in? Let her go or watch her fuckin' skull crack in my hands?* He swallowed, feeling the sweat beading on his forehead. Dr. Thibideaux would not approve of him losing his cool like this, and the last thing Nico wanted was to disappoint his mentor. He had worked too hard to get to a peaceful place. A place without nightmares, screaming, and hot, sticky blood... *woosah*!

He wasn't going to turn back now. *Calm the beast, Nico*, he could hear his doctor saying in that soothing voice that always seemed to make the world alright again. Besides, he would *have* to calm himself. Dr. Thibideaux wasn't there to administer *thorzine* to him this time, sedating him to the point of sleeping for three days straight. No- this time he'd have to take control of his own temper.

He took a deep breath with difficulty, cleared his throat, and slowly pried his fingers away from his wife's arm.

"Why," he managed to choke out in a voice that sounded strangely desperate. "Why are you doing this?"

Marielle took a deep breath feeling vindicated, but sad somehow.

"Come on, Nico. You have to know that our lives together ended the first time that you cheated on me and the dozens of times after that. You haven't been a husband to me. You have sex with woman after woman and then come home and look me in the eyes like you haven't done a thing. And I know that it isn't just sex because I do my best to give you sex. Might be vanilla sex in your eyes, but I try to at least perform my wifely duties. No- it's more than that. You have actual relationships with some of these women... the one they say is a singer.

"I know she's special to you. I know you've promised her the same things you've promised me- a life together with children and happiness. But I'm your wife, Nico, and she's nothing but a mistress. I can't wrap my mind around how you could promise her the same things that you promised your wife. To be honest, I'm tired of trying to figure it out. I'm just amazed that you even have the balls to stand there and face me knowing that I know all you've done."

Nico's sweaty hands trembled as his fists clenched and unclenched. He began to rock back and forth, doing his best to comfort himself. Maybe he *did* still need the *thorzine*.

"You're a tyrant- a violent man with severe emotional and psychological problems. For ten years, I've turned a blind eye. Ten years, I allowed you access to my money to do what you would with it thinking that maybe there was something there between you and I that could be salvaged… that maybe one day you would wake up and see what you have right in front of you and we could be how we were in the beginning."

She sighed, paused, and continued.

"But no, it was never me you wanted. It was always the money and the lifestyle. I was never anything to you but some kind of trophy. And no matter how much I give or how much I love or how much I cater, I'm never going to be enough. Life with me just isn't enough for you. It just isn't in you to give a damn about me one way or the other, and it's time I face that reality. You don't love me, have never loved me, and you're never going to love me. I never should have married you knowing that."

"That's not true, Mari!" Nico shouted insolently stamping his foot. "I love… I mean I really do love… I feel very intensely… for… We're married, Mari! And when you marry you make a commitment until death do you part! I love… our marriage! You're just being mean!"

Nico heard the words leave his mouth with difficulty, knowing they probably sounded foreign and false rolling around in the ears of his wife, but he had to say something to keep her from leaving him.

He knew that he looked confused because he felt it. He couldn't remember a time when he'd ever told his wife that he loved her. *Did he love her? He did love her, right? What is love? Did he even know? Of course he did. He loved... something. He loved... what did he love?* The thoughts raced through his mind leaving burning holes of uncertainty like sharp, repetitive bullets.

Marielle shook her head feeling that she had no choice but to continue.

"Listen, I may be passive, but I'm not an idiot. There's not a single scrap of love in your body for me... never has been and never will be. You think I don't know that? Every month you come up with a new scheme to get yourself out of the house so you can screw every woman in the French Quarter while I sit out here in the country waiting for you to come home. Now you've gone and cooked up some type of political career scheme thinking I'm really going to buy that mess. You and I both know that there is no political career. You need help. Don't you see you're delusional? How do you expect me to stay married to you when you don't even have good sense? Maybe the doctor who helped you before, Dr. Thibideaux, could-"

"Marielle, have you lost your *entire* mind," Nico demanded, his voice booming through the parlour with his hands clenched in tight fists as the calm he had been trying to maintain began to crack like ice. "What the hell are you talking about?"

Marielle shook her head in amazement.

"Imagine *you* asking *me* if I've lost my mind when *you're* the one running around town nuttier than a fruitcake talking about a campaign that doesn't even exist."

"It *does* exist! Why can't you just support me like wives should do for their husbands? Instead you're talking down to me just like my mother used to do!"

"Oh don't even try to bring your mother into this, Nicodemus! I'm nothing like her. I've supported you through every scheme and through every affair. But no more of that stupidity. You have to stop this now. You can't continue with this charade."

"It's not a charade! It's *not* a charade. My career is real!"

"Fine. If this fake political campaign for Senator is actually real, tell me what party are you associated with? Are you a Democrat or a Republican?"

"What?" Nico asked confused, feeling put on the spot. "What do you mean asking me that, Mari? Huh? You think you can degrade me with your high powered university logic?"

"This isn't about degradation, Nico. It's a real question. What party are you running for? Do you even know? Or did you think just running around town shouting that you will be Senator to anyone who will listen will actually get you on the ballot?"

"No! I *do* know my party and I *will* be Senator! Ballot be damned! I'm a Democratic Republican if you must know! See! You don't even know about that, Mari! You don't even know what a Democratic Republican does!"

"I sure don't! I don't think anybody does!"

"I'm going to change this state and then later on, the country! And then you'll be sorry! You'll be sorry you doubted me!"

Marielle threw up her hands.

"Do you even hear yourself, man? That doesn't make a lick of sense! You're insane! Do you have any control over how creepy you allow yourself to get?"

"I'm not insane *or* creepy! I'm distinguished! A gentleman! And maybe ever a scholar!"

Marielle sighed and shook her head.

"Listen, I know that this is coming as a sudden shock to you, but this is effective immediately. I want you out of my house tonight. I can't stand another minute of this life. You have no concept of reality and this has to end-now."

Nico could feel the rage in the pit of his stomach bubbling like boiling water. It seared through his intestines, making him feel like his ass was on fire. His body twitched involuntarily as the horrific monster in his gut neared the surface. If she got him so angry that he shit his pants, he was going to rip out her eyes and scramble them like eggs. *Hold on to yourself, Nico… don't let the beast take over*, he could hear Dr. Thibideaux say. *Just breathe.*

He looked at his wife who in truth was much more beautiful than his mistress. She was much more prim and proper… conservative and classy. She was the perfect Southern Belle… the perfect wife for a future Senator like himself. Maybe if he reasoned with her, she'd change her mind and no damage would have to be done to her.

He swallowed, held his burning stomach, and tried to compose himself before his bowels released. Because if they did release and he shit himself, there'd be fiery hell to pay.

"Where do you expect me to go, Marielle? This is my home… the home I've made with you for over a decade. You're my family- the only family I've got!"

Marielle tilted her head back and laughed.

"Ha! Home my ass! This is *my* family's house, and I want you gone. That makes it *my* home. You think I give a damn where you go? I suggest you make an appointment with a psychiatrist and get yourself some help. Then get your shit and get out! Rent a car, a room, whatever it is you need to survive, but get your lying, cheating, crazy ass out of here! I'm not going to live like this anymore. It's over!"

That's it! Nico's fury peaked and burst, overflowing like a volcanic pimple under pressure as each word crashed down over him in waves of madness blacker than midnight. He lashed out in one quick breath and smacked Marielle so hard that spit and blood flew from her mouth in red foam as she bit down on her tongue and collapsed to the floor.

He grabbed her, growling like a rottweiler, and slammed her into the wall with such force that hanging pictures and books on the shelves crashed to the floor. He threw a quick punch that whistled through the air and served to blacken and swell Marielle's eye in an instant, fracturing some of the bones in her face. Then another punch, and another, until her face was knotted up like a rope.

Breathing hard with his chest heaving like a gorilla's and sweat beading on his brow, he wrapped his thick hands tightly around her soft neck and squeezed until her eyes bulged from her head.

"*Bouzin*[28]! Didn't you hear me tell you that this shit was forever? Didn't I tell you that this was 'til death do us part, Marielle? Didn't I? Huh? Huh? Fuckin' answer me!"

---

[28] *Bouzin*- bitch; slut in Creole (Kreyol)

He could barely get the words out; he was so out of breath. Spit flew from his mouth in thick, white globs with each word he spat at her.

"You're trying to trash my career now, you bitch! You're trying to destroy this marriage? Trying to end everything I've worked so fuckin' hard for! Do you know what it took for me to be in this marriage with you for ten years with your dry ass, sand paper, pussy? You bitch! You fuckin' high school cunt! I told you I loved you didn't I? I fuckin' said I love this marriage! This shit is for fuckin' ever! You will *never* leave me! *Never*!"

Marielle's eyes rolled into the back of her head. Everything was fading to black- fast. He was really going to do it… he was really going to kill her this time. Nico watched with wild eyes and bared teeth as he tightened his grip, wanting to snap her neck. If he just snapped her neck, everything would be okay. Just one little snap…

"You're gonna die, Mari! You're gonna die if you leave me! I'm going to kill you, you lying bitch! You probably fucked Pierre! I know you fucked Pierre didn't you? Didn't you? Tell me!"

He punched her again, this time crushing the bones in her nose. Thick blood poured in streams out of both nostrils. Before she could fall to the floor, his hands were right back around her neck, squeezing the life out of her.

"Admit it! You fucked Pierre! You sucked his big black dick! I knew you were a whore! You're a high school whore with long hair and pretty clothes!"

Suddenly a blinding flash in his mind brought him to his knees as a pain so sharp, it reminded him of lightning seemed to strike his head. He groaned in pain, suddenly feeling light headed. In an instant, Nico was back in his childhood.

CHAPTER II

"Nico! Nico, don't hurt her! Stop! You have to stop!"

Nicodemus could see his little brother, Lucien, with the same scared look on his face he always wore whenever he'd lose control. He stepped away from the body ashamed that his brother had caught him at it again. He didn't want to meet his brother's eyes so instead focused on the girl's blank, dead, stare.

"You're supposed to live up to our ancestor's name, Nico! He was a holy man and a kind man! He didn't do stuff like this! You've got to stop doing this before they have you put away! No more bodies!"

"Please don't be mad at me, Lucien. Don't you see? I had to do it! She had a Magnolia in her hair just like Maman[29] wears. I had to-"

---

[29] *Maman- mama, mother in Creole (Kreyol)*

"No! You're doing it again! You promised you wouldn't! You lied to me! All you do is lie!"

"I never lied, Lucien! Maybe I fibbed a little but that's not a lie!"

Lucien shook his head, afraid of his brother.

"You're crazy, Nico! You've got to be stopped!"

"No, Lucien! You've got it all wrong, man! Everything is okay, really! Don't worry. I'm getting better control of it. This was just a little slip. Anybody can have a slip. I just saw the Magnolia and lost it for a minute, but I've got it back now. I'm okay. See? Look at me. Don't I look okay to you?"

Lucien shook his head, eyeing the dead girl on the ground with scared eyes.

"No, you're definitely not okay, Nico. Nothing about this is okay. You're getting worse. Somebody's gotta be the responsible one around here. Let me tell Maman so she can help you. She'll know what to do."

"No! Maman will put me back in the well! It's raining, Lucien! I'll drown! You know that she hates me! She thinks I'm evil! Then she'll call Father Mereaux and he'll try to touch me! Please, just let me get rid of the girl! We'll bury her in the swamp. No one will ever know. Don't tell on me, Lucien! Please! I need you. I'm getting better, I promise. It was just a slip. I'm gonna be a good man just like Nicodemus, our ancestor, and make Maman

proud so she won't put me in the well! We just have to keep this one secret. Please, Lucien, I'm begging you."

"No, Nico. This has to end. There's too much blood on your hands now. You've hurt too many people. You've even hurt-"

"Don't you say it! You know that was an accident!"

Nico stared at his brother with tears in his eyes feeling desperate. Was he losing his brother's love too? His mother already hated him. Lucien wouldn't meet his brother's eyes.

"Lucien, you know I'm sorry.   You're all I have. If you turn your back on me, I'll die! I just know it! Please just give me a chance to make things right. This girl was just a slip. I'm cured. I really am. I won't do it again."

"Just this once, you promise, Nico? No more bodies?"

"I promise! I'm better now. Just don't tell Maman."

Marielle grew limp in his arms like a corpse as the flashback faded to black. He blinked, feeling dizzy and nauseous. Fuckin' women always made him kill them! *It's their own fault*, he thought.

He looked at Marielle, feeling pure hatred for her... hatred mixed with a confused admiration that could be nurtured into love if given more time. After all, it had only been ten years. That really wasn't that long.

Her face had gone from red to ashen just that quickly and her lips had lost their color. An intense, cold, fear that he hadn't felt in years gripped Nico's heart suddenly. His stomach still bubbled with his anger, threatening to fill his pants with steamy fecal matter. *What the fuck did I just do*, he asked himself as he began to panic. *What the fuck did I just do to Marielle?*

He looked down at his hands wondering how he could be so damn stupid? Marielle's body crumpled to the floor beside her fallen Magnolia blossom with a loud thud. She had dark red handprints around her yellow neck… his handprints… and a grotesquely swollen, knotted up face that no one would even recognize. God, it had been *years* since he'd lost control like that! And now he'd made another mess. *Fuck! Lucien was just going to love this.*

"Mari," he called softly, almost afraid to touch her. His hands trembled as he smoothed a stray tendril of hair away from her face delicately. "Mari, wake up baby. Come on, get up for Daddy."

He caressed her puffed, broken, face tenderly feeling a wave of intense regret. He leaned down and kissed her busted lips, tasting some of her blood. It tasted strangely good as the salty, slightly metallic tasting droplets spread over his tongue.

"Mari, are you dead, baby? Come on. Tell me you're not dead. Tell Daddy. Just say the words."

He waited, but no response. He kissed her again, this time with tongue so he could taste more of her blood. It made him feel closer to her when he could taste it.

"I said tell me, baby. Tell Daddy."

Nico's intestines pulsed in pain as his anus began to burn trying to hold it all in. Oh God, his sphincter surely wouldn't hold it all. He could feel the muscles quivering, struggling not to let go. It was a reaction that happened every time he had gone too far. Dr. Thibideaux said that it was his body's way of dealing with the remorse he felt for the sins he'd committed- for the lives he'd taken. His body felt that it needed to suffer just like his victims suffered. But looking at Marielle now, his regret melted and his anger intensified… and so did his need to shit. He growled like a mad man.

"Bitch, you're doing this shit on purpose! You don't want me to succeed! You're jealous of me! You were always jealous of me because I look good! Because I have a career and all the ladies want me! Now you're gonna try to die on me so you can get me into some trouble? Get your trifling ass up before I kill you again!"

He shook her hard then punched her broken face again, drawing more blood, adding more damage. Still no response...

"This can't be happening! Why won't you wake the fuck up? You selfish cunt! You were always a selfish bitch, Marielle! Always! And now you're trying to die!"

Nico could feel himself growing more and more worked up. His vision was still blurry and the muscles in his ass twitched as he worked hard not to shit himself.

"Fuckin' breathe! I swear if you don't breathe, I'll fuck you up! That's a promise, Mari! You hear me? Huh? You want that?"

He waited, but was met with no response.

"So you ain't gon' answer, bitch?"

Nico shook her with brute strength, but Marielle was as limp as a dishrag. Her head bobbed around like a rag doll's. What was he going to do, now? She was no good to him dead. Besides, he'd promised Lucien 20 years ago, no more bodies. How was he going to explain his wife's lifeless body lying on the floor?

"Fuckkkk!" he screamed as he repeatedly beat the sides of his head with his fists, bruising and assaulting his own skin until it was purple and dark. His busted knuckles were bloody and raw. "Not happening! *Not fuckin' happening*!"

His stomach gave one last, strong, heave as he doubled over in pain. His breathing had gone from hard to exhausted making that *huh-huh-huh* sound as he struggled to swallow the last bit of spit in his mouth.   He swayed on his feet, feeling dizzy. It was coming! He couldn't hold it any longer! His sphincter gave away and the muscles relaxed as his burning anus opened up wide and released his bowels everywhere. The room instantly filled with the thick, sickening smell of burning rubber and rotten food. The fecal matter streamed down the side of his legs and out the bottom of his pants like watery mud making a shit paste on the floor.

"No!" he screamed and fell dramatically to the floor in a fit of tears kicking his feet like a child. "Not again! I didn't do it! It wasn't me! *Maman*, please don't throw me down the well! I'm sorry! Lucien! Help! She's gonna drown me in the well! Noooo! Please! I don't want to go see Father Mereaux!"

He sat there for over fifteen minutes crying his eyes out and stinking in a shitty mess. He kicked his feet and beat his head and even howled like a coyote as if he were in extreme pain, berating himself for what he'd done to Marielle.

Still, he knew that he couldn't stay there like that. He did have sense enough to realize that. Charlize, the head maid in the house, would come early in the morning and she'd certainly have a lot to say about a dead body on the middle of the floor... particularly the dead body of the Lady of the House. Not to mention her employer sitting in a pile of runny shit would probably make a big stink. He had no other choice but to get it together and form a plan.

What else could he do? If he continued to sit there, he'd be hauled off to jail before dawn.

Reluctantly, he calmed himself. His hands trembled as he took out his cell phone and smudged brown residue all over the screen as he tried to dial. Desperate times called for desperate measures.

"Yeah, it's me. I've - I've got a bit of trouble. And before you panic, I just want you to know it wasn't my fault! I need you to come out here to the house, and bring the truck. Don't ask me any questions! Can't you see I'm distraught? This is no time to judge me! And for the record, I don't appreciate your sarcastic tone!"

CHAPTER III

"Throw her in the water. The 'gators will take care of the rest. And hurry up, will ya? I don't like being an accessory to murder!"

"Wait a minute, here. I can't just throw her in the water. We've gotta cut off her head, hands, and maybe her feet so that if they do find her, they can't identify her! You know the 'gators won't eat everything and there could still be some pieces left! I don't want anyone to ever find out who she is."

"Are you crazy? You think we've got all night or something? We've got to get out of here before someone realizes she's missing. You'll be the first person that they suspect. We need to establish an alibi. Just throw her in the water so we can go. It's creepy out here!"

"What if she drifts to shore? We're not that far out in the water! We've been driving next to the shore this whole time!"

"Nico, she's fuckin' dead! What difference does it make if she drifts to shore? We're in the middle of the damn bayou! Nobody is going to find her! Now toss her and let's go."

"Alright, I guess you're right. I'm sorry, Lucien. I didn't mean to drag you into this again. Will you forgive me? Not just for this, but for all my sins?"

"Now you know damn well that I can't just tell you to say a hail Mary and all is forgiven. You've really fucked up this time. And you still haven't lived up to the name Maman gave you. All you're doing is making a huge mess, racking up bodies. Maman and Father Mereaux were right about you. You're just a screw up and on top of that, you're evil. You're pure evil, Nico- a curse on this family."

"No! That's not true! I've always been sorry for everything. I never meant to hurt anyone. I'm going to be Senator of Louisiana soon, Lucien. You'll see. I'll make a great name for our family just like our ancestor did. Just believe in me. I'm doing it for you. Don't you believe in me?"

"Hell nah! Don't even start me to lying. I don't believe a word you're saying."

"But- but you have to! You're all I have left, Lucien! You have to believe in me... you just have to!"

Marielle swore she could hear those words spoken by a distant, muffled voice- a voice so desperate, that she almost felt sorry for it. It was like a bad dream. She remembered, or at least she thought she remembered, being attacked by Nico, but then again, she wasn't sure. Maybe she'd dreamt it all. Wouldn't be the first time she'd dreamt of him hurting her.

The only thing that was different about this time though, was the pain. Her face and head were throbbing so badly that it felt like her head had been smashed over and over again into a brick wall! Her throat felt so tight and swollen that she could barely get any breath.

She could feel the blood from her mouth dried all over her face, making her skin sticky and clammy as mosquitos buzzed around. She tried to pry open her swollen eyes, but they seemed so heavy, excruciatingly painful, and bloody. When she was finally able to take a peek through the slits that were now her eyes, everything looked blurry and out of focus like a camera lens cloudy with water. It was all a strange collage of muddied greens, blacks, and reds.

They were moving- the soft but steadily propelled motion that you feel when you're on a boat. She could hear the guttural sputter of the motor and the soft lapping of the water along its sides. Her hands clumsily fumbled around feeling the cold steel of the boat's floor and she knew then that they were down the bayou.

She tried to part her bloodied, cracked lips to ask where she was, but her throat was so dry and tight that no sound would come out.

"There! Throw her there!"

Suddenly a set of massive hands yanked Marielle up and flung her like garbage into the mucky waters of the swamp. Still unable to move much, the dead weight of her body hit the water with a gigantic splash and began to sink into the murky depths with mire clinging to her clothes and hair. And just as quickly, the soft sputtering of the little boat became louder and more aggressive as it took off at high speed in the opposite direction.

Marielle's breath caught in her closed throat as salty water filled her mouth and nostrils. She gasped and coughed. "Help!" she screamed in a strained whisper as her head dipped under the water and back up again. "Somebody help me, please!"

Fear pumped through her veins like heroin, as the prospect of drowning became a real threat. The adrenaline made her feel jittery and unstable, but then was not the time to pay attention to that. With her limbs barely working and her face feeling like her head had been smashed into a wall, maybe it would have been kinder to just give up and just allow herself to drown. Death was easier. The problem with that was that she'd never been a quitter before and she damn sure wasn't about to start being one. Besides, she needed to live long enough to watch her husband scream from the depths of his balls in agony after she made him pay for what he'd done to her.

She struggled desperately to keep herself afloat, even though she was freezing thanks to all the blood she'd loss, not to mention the blinding pain shooting through her body. *How am I going to get out of this? What do I do*, she racked her brain over and over.

And just as if fate heard her and wanted the last laugh, she spotted the distinct lumps of a brown and black log drifting steadily towards her. *Now that's just what the hell I need... more danger*, she thought to herself.

In the swamp, a log is never a log. Everybody knows that. When you think you see a log in the swamp, it's your best bet to get the hell out of dodge before you become intimately familiar with the dietary tract of an alligator.

It was time for survival mode. Marielle kicked away as hard as she could, doing her best not to panic. She wanted to scream her head off and thrash all over the place, but losing her head like that would cost her, her life.

Plants with curling tendrils seemed to wrap themselves around her body like they had a mind of their own, dragging her underneath the disgusting water. As she dipped below the surface again just before mud caked up in her swollen slits for eyes, a water moccasin slithered past her looking for something to sink its fangs into.

"ARRRRRRRRRGH!" she screamed under the water unable to stand the terror that she felt as the nastiness of the swamp filled her mouth again, nearly drowning her.

As if an alligator and drowning wasn't enough, a water moccasin, which was nothing but a fancy name given to the pit viper native to swampy waters, could give her the most painful snake bite on earth, and maybe end it all in a matter of seconds. And if he didn't end it all, he was for damn sure going to take off a chunk of her leg thanks to his necrosis inducing venom.

So which was worse? Being eaten alive by an alligator, drowning in the mucky, thick, brown water of the swamp, or rotting from the inside out thanks to a damn snake bite? *Don't panic! Don't panic,* she told herself over and over again as her heart beat wildly in her chest like a horse racing for the stables. It beat so hard and fast that it almost felt lodged in her throat.

The day sure had turned on her. She'd gone from having the upper hand and filing for divorce at a lawyer's office, ready to get rid of her crazy ass husband, to finding herself nearly beaten within an inch of her life and left for dead in the waters of the bayou. She could taste a black, bitter, bile vomit itself into her mouth, spread across her tongue, and make her newfound hate for Nico hotter than the flames of hell.

She vowed mercilessly to God- the Devil- whoever was listening, that if she ever got her ass out of that bayou alive and in one piece, her dear husband would suffer the worst type of agony imaginable: enslavement of the soul. If he really wanted to try to kill somebody and leave them to rot in a swamp, she'd have to show his ass what killing somebody was really all about.

She popped back up above the water and took a big gasp of air, rejuvenated with the will to live if only to see Nico die. She would have to make it out alive in order to do that, so she began to regroup her thoughts. She knew she had to swim as fast as she could before the snake recoiled at her and the alligator sped up to snap her body in half. She dived back under the water feeling weak, but couldn't afford to give out. She forced her body to move forward.

She couldn't see a damn thing. The waters were too murky and filled with sludge that seeing anything other than darkness was an impossibility. All the same, she knew she needed to go the opposite direction of the danger if she didn't want the bayou to be her last chapter. She struggled to push her way through the water, as turtles and other animals flitted past her. She could have sworn a Gar snapped at her feet... thankful that it missed. Anybody who has ever seen an archaic looking Gar (probably a cousin of some aquatic dinosaur), knows you don't want that thing snapping at your feet.

A Great Blue Heron swooped down, with its majestic wings, to catch a fish. And just as he spotted his target, he ducked his piercing, sharp, beak into the water right into Marielle's thigh.

"ARRRRRRRRRGH!" she screamed as the pain shot up her leg in cold jolts and blood gushed from the wound in spurts.

If she didn't get out of the water now, she'd really be dead meat soon. It would only take seconds before the alligator got a whiff of the blood, and that would be all she wrote. She scrambled frantically forward and felt her heart leap for joy as she reached the soft ground of the bayou banks. She clambered clumsily ashore, her feet sinking in the muck of the soaked ground and raced her way through the cypress trees, desperate to get away from the alligator.

Out of breath and body aching, Marielle collapsed on the soft ground. She was breathing so hard that her lungs burned. She looked back to the dark waters only to find the alligator with mouth wide, sharp teeth bared, ready to storm her and make her a meal once he got to land.

"Oh my God! Help!" she screamed, her throat raw as she climbed to her feet. "Leave me alone!"

What the hell was she going to do now? *Damn you, Nicodemus*, she thought bitterly to herself. She felt so terrified that she was almost too shaky to run. She fell to the ground again, grabbing at anything she could use as a weapon. The alligator was rushing towards her with its stubby little legs going double quick.

"Hail Mary, full of grace," she started as she grabbed a thick, fallen branch.

The alligator lunged like a hungry predator, snapping its massive jaws at her legs, hoping to land a bit of flesh between his razor sharp teeth.

"The Lord is with thee-" she continued breathlessly, her voice quivering with fear as pee streamed down her leg uncontrollably, stinging the nasty stab wound from the Blue Heron.

Though she was trembling and feeling like she was in the twilight zone, Marielle swung with all of her might, cracking the alligator right across the eyes like she was Joe DeMaggio. Splinters from the wood broke off into the scaly eyelids, temporarily blinding the giant lizard... thoroughly pissing him off. Angry and wounded, the alligator made a grisly, hissing, cry and snapped its massive jaws again, this time just missing Marielle's arm. She knew that it wouldn't stop coming for her... at least not until her body lie in a hundred bloody, half eaten pieces.

"Blessed are those amongst women, and blessed is the fruit of thy womb Jesus-"

CRACK! She swung again, this time jabbing the alligator through its nostril and drawing blood as the splintered wood pierced through its scaly skin and came out on the other side. Blood oozed down its muzzle as it snapped viciously. She'd really pissed him off now. It snapped so close to Marielle's leg this time that she could feel its hot, rancid breath on her skin. Catching a bit of her weapon within its jaws, it rolled over and over like a monster in the mud, thinking it had bitten Marielle. It wanted to break her neck. She squealed in fear as adrenaline pumped through her veins.

"Holy Mary, Mother of God, pray for us sinners now and at the hour of our death! Now die you ugly fucker!"

Marielle gave the monstrous alligator a final stab through its eyeballs with her splintered branch, sending blood and soft eye tissue squirting everywhere. The monster seemed to howl and hiss in pain, shaking its head from side to side and rolling in the mud trying to get the wood out.

Marielle didn't waste any time. She ran as fast as her stabbed leg would allow her to hobble, fighting her way through hanging, Spanish Moss. She ran for as long as she could and finally collapsed on the ground out of breath in agonizing pain. The wound where the Blue Heron had stabbed her was still oozing blood, but she didn't even have the strength to tie a tourniquet. Even though she'd miraculously gotten away from that alligator, she was still in terrible danger.

It was dark now and the mosquitos were buzzing. Not only was she still in danger from the wild life in the swamp, she was also in danger of contracting Yellow Fever, Malaria, or even West Nile. Even so, she was exhausted and just didn't have the strength to go any further. Her leg wouldn't allow her to move anymore. The throbbing was so intense that she was beginning to feel delirious and close to unconsciousness. She collapsed on the soft, green, velvety moss breathing heavily and listening to the grasshoppers, cicadas, and tree frogs make their nighttime music.

She held on to the distant hope that some Cajun, bayou man paddling along in a pirogue[30] who had come out to fish, would find her and save her. She knew the probability of that was slim to none. Anyone who lived down the bayou wasn't often out on the waters after dark. The night was a treacherous time to be out in the swamp.

Tears streamed down her cheeks as she sobbed with fear and hatred. With her situation growing more desolate by the minute, she couldn't help but think of her obviously psychotic husband. He had been the one to put her there. Everything that she was going through was because of him. He'd beaten her to a pulp just as if she were a man and had then left her in the wild to die. Her blood boiled and she itched to dig her long nails into his eyeballs, scratching them blind. And suddenly her grandmother's words seemed to whisper in her ears in that

---

[30] Pirogue- a small, flat bottomed boat similar to a canoe

familiar accented voice that always made her feel safe as a child. It was no louder than the hushed murmur of a stream, but clear as crystal just the same.

"Hush that crying! You know just what to do. Invoke the secrets of your ancestors, ti petit fi mwen[31]. Invoke the secrets of Bizango and know your revenge! Remember!"

The words drifted on the sigh of a sudden, soft breeze- a sweet, welcomed break from the heat and humidity of the swamp. As a mosquito nibbled at her ear and the drunken heat slackened her body,   slowly, her heavy eyelids closed and she saw relaxed blackness. Her grandmother's words still lingered in her ear.

"Remember!"

---

[31] *Ti petit fi mwen-* Creole (Kreyol) for "my little girl; my little one"

CHAPTER IV

Flowers. There were so many different types of flowers surrounding the bed. Tulips, Orchids, and Callalilies- a beautiful floral arrangement. There were even several fresh bouquets of South African Bird-of-Paradise flowers with their bright array of blue, orange, and a pinch of red- one of her favorites. But white Magnolia blossoms, of course, were her absolute favorite.

He had spared no expense on the arrangements, hoping to convey to the public that he was, indeed, a loving husband. After all, the public would love to elect a man to the Senate who stood faithfully by his wife as she lay in the hospital recovering from a horrific ordeal. It showed that he was a Family Man and made him seem sympathetic.

The thick, sweet, floral scent swirled through the air transforming the sterile, hospital room to a somewhat happier place. The sound of the breathing machine breathing and heart monitors beeping didn't seem so bad

when there were flowers around. At least Nico hoped that
the public would see it that way if they ever bothered to
see what their future Senator was up to. Never know when
a spontaneous photo op would arrive.

"It's not definite, as there is always a chance
however it is beginning to look as if she may not wake up,
Mr. LaCroix. During the weeks we've had her here her
recovery has been stagnant at best. There hasn't been even
the slightest change, good or bad. The Yellow Fever left
her in quite a weakened state out in the bayou. As you can
imagine, Yellow Fever with delayed medical attention can
be a very formidable condition."

Nico nodded his head listening, hoping that the
doctor would get to the point. He was late for a campaign
event, after all.

"There really wasn't much that we could do other
than sustain her life. I'm afraid Mrs. LaCroix will likely
require life support for the remainder of her days and will,
in turn, deteriorate the longer she remains in a coma.
We've done all we can for the moment. All we can do
now is wait and see if she comes out of it."

Nicodemus looked down into Marielle's beautiful
face, with his lips twitching to crack a smile. Though her
skin was pale and clammy, she still held all of the beauty
that was notorious in the women of the Blanchard family.
Now all of that beauty would wither away and die. Still, at
least he hadn't out right killed her and now Lucien
couldn't say he'd added another body to the list.

"Mr. LaCroix, there is one more pressing matter that accompanies Mrs. LaCroix's condition, I'm sorry to say. And I would like you to know that I apologize for having to address this issue when you're going through so much right now."

Nico looked up at the doctor with the messy blonde hair who was dressed in his white lab coat.

"And that is?"

"Well, I'm sorry to say, but Mrs. LaCroix's insurance will not pay for continuous life support. I'm afraid the expenses will be considerable. The hospital will need you to sign papers stating that you will be held accountable for payment or-"

"No need for that. I'd like to terminate life support, Doctor," he said with a wave of his hand.

The doctor frowned, unsure if he'd heard the man correctly.

"Come again?" the doctor asked.

"I said that I want to terminate my wife's life support- immediately. Sustaining life support will cost me a fortune and you've already told me that there's nothing more you can do. There's no need to drag this thing out any longer, prolonging my wife's suffering. I want to give Marielle some peace. Besides, I have my campaign to worry about. I really can't be bothered with this."

"Uh… uh… your campaign?"

"That's right. Lots of really cool stuff like speeches and kissing babies and visiting little old ladies in the nursing home. Gotta get the old folks' vote, ya know. Can't make Senator without 'em."

The doctor blinked in confusion while Nico stood there giving him a winning smile with deep dimples.

"Uh… okay… well, uh… we can do as you wish, Mr. LaCroix. It's your call, really. I just thought you might want to wait a little longer to see if your wife would make any progress. This all just seems so sudden."

"Sudden? It's been weeks. If the ole girl hasn't awakened yet, I'm pretty sure we can call it a day and move on, right? I've made my peace with this, Doc. Trust me. I was never very good at marriage anyway. Please draw up the necessary papers and have them sent to me for signature. I will, of course, require a copy of the death certificate as well. You may contact the Blanchard family for her interment because really, I'm no good with funerals. Dead bodies, people crying, ycch! The whole thing gives me the creeps. I'm sure her family would want to be in charge of that anyway. They can come up from Haiti and handle it."

Nico said the words icily, and the doctor's neck hairs stood on end. He shivered.

"Oh, and uh Doc, one last thing. If we could keep this little conversation between me and you... I mean, I really wouldn't like to have this heartbreaking decision swaying the vote of the People, you know? Sympathy votes and all- just wouldn't be right. Best to keep things low key."

The doctor frowned, confused.

"Uh... Mr. LaCroix, are you sure that this is what you really want? This seems a rash choice. Maybe you might like to take the time to think about this before you make any permanent decisions."

Nico grabbed his wife's clammy hand and kissed it, letting his tongue lick over her skin once or twice, tasting her sweat. The doctor watched, horrified. *What in the world is wrong with this man*, he wondered to himself. Still holding Marielle's hand to his mouth looking like he was about to bite her, Nico stared at the doctor with black eyes.

"Please excuse us, Doc, would ya? I'd like to say goodbye to my wife properly. This is very hard for me and I need my wife to know how much I love her. She would have wanted it this way. My sweet Marielle... She would want me to go on with my life and my campaign. I'm doing this for her, you know? When I'm Senator, it'll all be in her honor. She was such a do-gooder and now I will be too."

The blonde doctor looked warily at his patient. She would be dead soon on his orders thanks to her husband. The doctor shuddered, feeling a cold chill creep down his spine.

"Well, I guess there's nothing more to say. I will do as you have instructed, Mr. LaCroix."

The doctor turned and walked out after giving one last sorrowful look at his patient. When he was finally gone, Nico looked down at Marielle as his lips spread into a ghoulish smile.

"Awful situation you find yourself in now, *chérie mwen*. Just awful. But, it's not like I didn't try to get you to listen. I mean, I tried to tell you. I told you that this thing between me and you was forever. Til' death do us part. Isn't that what the priest said when he married us?"

He chuckled, feeling in control.

"It looks like I've held up my end of the bargain, wouldn't you say? Death is coming for you very soon my love, and I'm parting."

He leaned down and kissed her cherry colored, plump lips, which the orderlies kept moist with lip balm. Such sweet, luscious lips... He certainly hadn't had the freedom to kiss them whenever he wanted before. He had wanted to kiss them, suck them, and bite them. He had wanted to pull them with his teeth. But every time he'd try, Marielle would scream that it hurt when he bit down on them. It always pissed him off. A little pain never hurt anybody.

But Marielle was always telling him no and to stop. She never let him control and dominate her the way a man should control his woman. She ate what she wanted, did what she wanted, and even talked to whomever she wanted. She made business deals and bought real estate without his consent. She even told him that they could only have sex once a day, and even then she wouldn't take it in the ass. What kinda shit was that for a wife to tell her husband? Won't take it in the ass? That alone was grounds for an ass whipping.

Now that she was in a coma, there was nothing that she could do about anything anymore. He could do anything to her- anything at all, and all she'd be able to do was lie there and take it like a good wife is supposed to.

He felt his penis harden instantly as he thought about all the things he could do to her without hearing her whining, nagging, and screaming about the pain. For once he could force her to be the type of wife she was supposed to be.

Marielle just lay there, saying nothing and seeing nothing but the back of her eyelids. Nico could feel the familiar heat of lust quicken his pulse as he stood staring at his beautiful wife. *So many things I can do*, he thought.

He reached out to touch the clammy skin on her arm and his own skin broke out in gooseflesh. Touching her was like touching an angel. And finally he could do it just the way he wanted. Anxious to do more than touch, he slowly and sneakily reached up under her bed sheets, his fingers creeping up her thighs and found her forbidden treasure. He glanced quickly at the door to make sure no one was coming, feeling more alive than he ever had at the prospect of finally having his wife. Then he dug his fingers inside of his prissy, conservative wife's hole and rubbed his thumb over her clit. It was pure electricity!

In the eight weeks she'd been in the hospital, no one had bothered to trim her pubic hairs. They grew bushy and wild, curling this way and that right off her lips like jungle vines. Just the feel of her wild hairs intertwining with each other in his hands made him so hard that he could barely stand it. The head of his penis throbbed with precum itching to be released.

"Oh yes, Mari. You're going to give me what I deserve as a husband. You fuckin' did your best to keep it away from me, didn't you? Ten fuckin' years of white washed sex only once a day! Well guess what, Marielle, it's mine now! You're going to be the slut I know you can be, now. I'm gonna tear your ass to pieces! You hear me?"

Nico pulled the covers all the way off, breathing excitedly like a bull and unbuckled his pants. He pulled out his long, thick penis that was so engorged with blood that it stood straight out with strong veins lining his shaft like vines running wild. He rolled Marielle over onto her side, lined himself up behind her, and thrust his hard dick inside of her with as much force as he could possibly muster.

"Get wet, you slut! Get wet and give it to me!" he yelled, pushing himself repeatedly inside Marielle who was dry enough to start a fire.

"You think I won't take it? You think I won't get it from you? Oh I 'm gonna get it! You can bet your sweet ass on that!"

Nico pounded Marielle over and over and over again, as her head bobbed around like a rag doll, banging up against the side of the hospital bed. He grunted and groaned, ooh'd and ahh'd, intoxicated with the way his helpless wife was unable to do anything about his dominance. He grabbed a handful of her hair and pulled it so hard that some of it came out in his hands. He stuffed some of the black curls into his nostrils, breathing in her smell. She smelled delicious, just like Magnolia blossoms. The smell made him feel drunk and obsessive. He darted his tongue in and out of her ear like a snake, tasting a bit of her earwax buildup.

"Ooooh, nasty girl. Dirty girl. I taste your dirty little secret."

His eyes rolled into the back of his head in ecstasy as he felt that uncontrollable sudden rush take over him.

"Oooooh, fuck you, Marielle! You bitch! You cunt! You whorrrrrrrrrrrrrrrrre!"

He busted inside of her, releasing everything he had never been able to give her before, then collapsed on top of her with a tired huff. It was the best he'd felt in years. And in a strange way, he felt closer to his wife now more than he ever had. It was the first intimate moment where he felt like maybe he might have loved his wife after all.

"You can be a wild girl when you want to be, Mari. I knew that you had it in you. You just needed me to help you."

Nico chuckled at his handy work and kissed her neck tenderly. Marielle's eyes remained closed. Nothing he'd done garnered any type of response from her.

"Too bad we couldn't always be this way. You're so beautiful. God, Marielle! You're the most beautiful woman I've ever seen!"

He covered her back up with the sheet, making sure to stage it as if nothing had ever happened, then zipped up his pants. The wetness from all the sex juice bled through the sheets.

"I'll miss you, Mari, my beautiful blossom. Give my best to God when you see Him, will ya?"

He reached out to the flower arrangements and picked a lovely, Magnolia blossom from the bunch. He smelled it, inhaling the powerful scent of lemon, creamy honey suckle, and vanilla. He then placed the blossom in her hair.

"Absolutely beautiful... Radiant…"

He turned to leave.

"Oh and Mari, make sure you don't give my pussy up to anybody else, okay? A Senator needs a faithful wife even in Death."

With that, he headed out of the room, never looking back at the woman he'd been married to for ten years. He left her there to die, but he certainly didn't feel good about it. There was almost the hint of a tear in his eye… almost. As he passed the doctor on his way down the hall he called out to him.

"Make sure I get the death certificate, will ya, Doctor? Oh and be sure to vote for Nicodemus LaCroix in the upcoming election for Senate. *Au revoi.*[32]"

Giving him the wink and the gun and a click of his tongue, Nico walked off whistling. His sentimental moment of momentary love for Marielle had passed. The doctor shook his head in confusion. *I know damn well it isn't election year*, the young doctor thought to himself as he watched Nico finally go.

---

[32] *Au revoi-* Creole (Kreyol) for goodbye

CHAPTER V

One month later…

    Aleera lounged leisurely on a chaise in the drawing room, sipping on a glass of whipped cream flavored vodka. In her mind, she was finally getting the 5-star treatment that she felt she so richly deserved. Sure, being an R&B singer had afforded her some luxury, but she hadn't had a hit in years and that shit was depressing. Truth be told, the little bit of money she was making wasn't enough to wipe her ass with. She would buy an *Hermes* bag (because how could she possibly be considered a New Orleans Celebutante if she didn't have an *Hermes* bag?) and a couple of gallons of vodka. That was it. That little bit would dry up all her finances for a month. Then she'd be caught out there trying to figure out her next step and bumming drinks from the bartender at the little corner bar next to her apartment.

The few shows she *did* book in local New Orleans taverns certainly weren't bringing in enough dough to maintain her lifestyle. Luckily for her, Nico had at least agreed to let her stay at the house so she wouldn't have to struggle to pay for her overpriced penthouse apartment anymore. Being three months behind on rent which totaled about $12,000, her landlord probably would have kicked her out any day. That would have been embarrassing, but Nico had come to the rescue. It was sheer dumb luck that he hadn't objected when she suggested moving in after the sudden death of his precious wife, Marielle.

Now, with him off in New Orleans all the time, campaigning for Senator or whatever the hell he did all day, she was usually left with the big, grandeur plantation house to herself. And though it was boring as hell out there with nothing but cicadas and crickets making their endless racket, Aleera had at least finally gotten her man from the paws of that stuck up prude that he had married... even if the bitch *did* have to die for her to get him.

"Will *Madame* require anything else," Charlize, the maid "assigned" to be her personal servant, asked as she brought in a tray with *café au lait* and a trio of *beignets* for Aleera. She sat it down on the coffee table.

Aleera could hear the attitude in Charlize's tone and if the bitch didn't check herself, she would find herself out on her ass faster than she could bat those long, curled lashes of hers. Aleera didn't like her anyway and she was damn sure gonna demand that Nico get rid of her ass.

Though Charlize waltzed around in the ugliest, plainest, maid's uniform in the world that looked like it had seen its heyday 100 years ago, it was obvious that she had a sexy body beneath it with curves in all the right places. Not to mention, her face was stunning with tight, chocolate, seemingly edible skin.

Aleera wrinkled her nose, letting her dislike for the maid boil into hatred. She'd be damned if a woman as pretty as Charlize was gonna stick around and take her man from her. Stealing men was *her* job.

"Actually I want my *beignets* out on the porch. It's too damn stuffy in here. Ain't ya'll ever heard of air conditioning?"

"Perhaps *Madame* isn't aware that they're predicting a storm today. The heat, you see. It gives us an awful lot of trouble out here during the summer. Summer storms been wrecking things out here for as long as I can remember. There's sure to be thunder, lightning, and a lot of rain. Wouldn't *Madame* prefer her afternoon snack-"

"Oh you must not have heard me, huh? Got a hearing problem or something?" Aleera asked sassily, glaring at Charlize. "I didn't ask you shit about the damn weather. I said I wanted my *beignets* out on the porch. When I want your opinion on the weather, I'll ask for it!

That's how it works when you're the maid and I'm the mistress."

"Exactly- the mistress," Charlize said barely audible under her breath.

"Whatchu say, girl?" Aleera asked with attitude.

The maid sighed in frustration, bit her lower lip, and picked up the tray to move it out onto the porch.

"I said very well, *Madame*. As you wish."

"Don't be mumbling up under your breath like I can't hear you either. I ain't with that shit. Oh and I want more than three *beignets,* too. I'm not some little skinny minnie like you, pecking at my food like a bird. Bring me some more. I don't know what you thought this was. I ain't Marielle with her stuck up ass. I need a real plate of doughnuts. And they better be hot, too."

Charlize rolled her eyes and clamped her mouth shut. It was getting harder and harder to ignore Aleera's rudeness.

"Oh is there a problem? You got something you want to say to me? Huh? Actin' like your ass ain't The Help or something. Better get your shit together before you find your ass out there on the unemployment line. And news flash, it's a recession, honey. Shit ain't sweet out there on them streets with no job."

"You ought to know," Charlize mumbled rolling her eyes. "Ain't like you got a job the first..."

Aleera stuffed another cherry in her mouth and washed it down with a bit more vodka, watching the maid chafe under her stare. Charlize clenched the tray to the point that the coffee cup trembled just a bit. She took a few deep breaths and swallowed, then finally replied more audibly, "will that be all *Madame?*"

"No, that's not all! Get my damn *beignets* before my coffee gets cold. Why the hell you still standing there? I ain't got all day. I rather have a real drink anyway. Everybody in here always drinking coffee all the damn time! I don't want that shit. I need something with some kick! Whatchu need to be doing is bringing me a shot of Patrón or something like that. I'm not trying to drink this weak ass coffee."

"Yes, *Madame.*"

Charlize turned quickly and stalked off, hating her new assignment to specifically attend to Aleera's needs. She actually preferred cleaning shitty toilets to being a servant to a gold digger like Aleera. She had no idea what the hell Mr. LaCroix was thinking assigning her to Aleera when he knew damn well they wouldn't get along. But who was she to argue? She was just The Help.

Her family had worked for the Blanchard Family for well over two hundred years even before they'd come to America from Haiti. She knew she would disgrace her mother and grandmother's memory if she were fired. She couldn't help but wonder if they would still care about her being fired considering Marielle- the last of the original Blanchards, was dead and in the ground now. But she knew it didn't matter one bit. She couldn't leave the house even if she wanted. The Blanchards had seen to that all those years ago. She would serve in that house until the end, and nothing Aleera did would stop it.

Still, she was tired of Aleera's shit and there wasn't much more that she was going to take. She may have been in a maid's uniform, but she wasn't the type to let some whore talk down to her like that. She was about ten seconds from putting a root on her ass- have her seeing some impossible shit she never thought she'd see. Maybe give her a few boils and a nasty wart right on her-

"Charlize! Where the hell are you with my *beignets*? You 'bout to piss me off, lollygagging and shit! You're on the clock! We ain't paying you to take all damn day!"

Charlize gritted her teeth and slammed the whole tray of *beignets* down on the ground. Aleera jumped at the crash of the shattered dishes. *No that bitch didn't!* She picked herself up from the chaise and marched over to Charlize like she was going to war.

"What the *fuck* is wrong with you, bitch? Are you *that* fuckin' clumsy that you can't carry a tea cup and saucer?"

Charlize took a deep breath and let the air out slowly.

"I apologize, *Madame*. Please forgive me. I-I-"

"You what? Huh?"

"I stumbled."

Aleera sneered at her, wanting to strike her. She looked her up and down, hating her petite yet curvy figure, and big, bright, doe eyes with long lashes.

"You stupid bitch," she spat bitterly. "Mr. LaCroix will hear about this when he gets home 'cause I don't have time for clumsy bitches. You can't clean worth shit either!"

Charlize said nothing, only counted the seconds hoping that Aleera would have sense enough to walk away. *Walk away, whore, before your whole world comes crashing down.*

"You did this shit on purpose didn't you? Breaking my man's good china! You can't even afford a spoon up in here, let alone all this shit you just broke! You ain't getting paid for today either so you can count that out. You're not going to disrespect me in my own house. I'll have you thrown out on your ass first!"

Charlize sighed and gave a polite smile.

"I'm sorry, *Madame*, but this is *not* your house. This home belongs to the Blanchards and it's only a matter of time before the remaining members of the family come and take it from Mr. LaCroix. When that happens, please believe the only person who will be thrown out on their ass is you. And even then, that's only if they're feeling generous which they're not inclined to be."

Aleera stood looking at her, stunned. Time passed quickly. One second... two seconds... three... Aleera drew her hand back and smacked Charlize so hard across the face that her head jerked to the right, putting a crook in her neck.

"Say that shit again, bitch! I dare you! I will beat the brakes off of your stupid ass! Ungrateful ass, disobedient, bitch! It's about to be a misunderstanding up in here 'cause I'll cut me a bitch! You got me all fucked up!"

Charlize readjusted her head and turned it slowly-eerily towards Aleera, twisting it at odd angles. Never taking her eyes off of Aleera, Charlize brought her fingers slowly to her lips and wiped away the trickle of blood that oozed there. The metallic taste spread across her tongue. Her eyes bored into Aleera's with a frightening fury that Aleera had never seen before; and the smallest pang of fear struck her in the chest like an arrow. Had she finally fucked with the wrong one?

For a split second, Charlize's face seemed to crumble and age right before Aleera's eyes, becoming creased with lines and drooping skin. What Aleera saw was no longer the petite beauty she'd just been arguing with, but a furious looking old woman with an evil fire in her ancient eyes. Aleera blinked and shook her head in confusion. Was her mind playing tricks on her? She swallowed and frowned, rubbing her eyes frantically. When she looked back at Charlize again, the maid looked completely normal and was still holding her hand to her mouth to stop the bleeding.

"Charlize?" Aleera asked confused.

"Something the matter, *Madame*? You look like you've seen a ghost. I can't imagine why you suddenly look so pale."

Aleera blinked again, unsure. Charlize looked like her normal, petite, beautiful self and stood smiling back at her politely despite her bloodied lip. Aleera took another sip of vodka and shook her head. Maybe she'd been drinking too much lately. She had been knocking them back pretty regularly not to mention she'd been taking Valium every now and again too. Drinking while taking pills probably *did* make you see things.

Suddenly the drawing room seemed to grow increasingly dark. Thick, grey clouds rolled over the sun and seemed to blot out the afternoon light. There was a low rumble of thunder that seemed to be growing closer with each passing second, making the moment more pregnant with tension. A storm was coming just like the maid had predicted. An eerie smile crept slowly across Charlize's bloody lips.

"You're cursed and don't even know it," she said in a voice so low that Aleera had to strain to hear her. "*Madame* Blanchard *will* have her revenge, make no mistake about that. And a scheming slut like you will get every last bit of what you deserve."

"What? What did you just say to me?"

"You heard me."

Aleera was itching to hit Charlize again. The fucking maid was threatening her! She wasn't gonna take that one lying down. Still, she felt her insides turn to ice. Something about her words seemed almost deadly. She staggered on her feet, feeling uneasy from all the vodka she'd drank.

"You're not worthy to be in this house," Charlize commented, observing her drunkenness.

"I'm gonna be the Lady of this house and you better learn to show me some fuckin' respect! I'm not gonna take too much more of you sassin' me when you ain't shit but a damn maid."

"You're going to die in this house. How's that for respect."

Aleera drew her hand back again, the ice cubes in her vodka clinking together. Charlize didn't flinch one bit. She held up two fingers and pointed them at Aleera unnervingly.

"As ye sow, so shall ye reap, *Madame*. You'd do well to remember that before you find yourself dreaming of death and the grave."

Lightning flashed illuminating the aged face of the old woman again. Aleera gasped. Charlize smiled politely with bleeding lips. Her face was normal.

"Enjoy the rest of your afternoon, *Madame*."

The maid walked calmly off, leaving Aleera confused with the spilled coffee and crumpled *beignets* on the floor.

Aleera swallowed. She'd been living down in Louisiana for the past ten years and was well aware of those hoodoo voodoo women, putting curses and spells on people. She didn't believe in any of that shit, but it was also the first time she'd ever had anyone talk to her like that. Not to mention the way she kept seeing the maid's face change. One minute she was beautiful and the next she was older than dirt. What the hell was *that* about?

She felt a tingling descend her spine that made her shudder with uneasiness. She stared at her glass of vodka. Maybe it was time to quit drinking.

She could feel her muscles trembling. She was really afraid. She rubbed the pimpled gooseflesh on her arms as she watched the sky grow even darker. The storm was just getting started.

CHAPTER VI

"Wow, Nico. She looks just like Marielle. I swear, it's uncanny. Is that why we followed her?"

Nico shhhed his brother angrily.

"Why are you so loud, Lucien, geez! Don't you know how to spy on somebody? You gotta be quiet."

"Spy? You can't be serious. I mean, what do you plan to accomplish by spying on this woman? Are you feeling tender about Marielle's death or something? Is that what this is all about?"

Nico rolled his eyes feeling annoyed.

"Damn it, can't you stop asking me questions for five measly minutes? I can't hear myself think!"

Lucien had no intentions of stopping.

"Think? Is that what you call yourself doing-thinking?"

"Ugh, shut up! You're such a judgmental fucker!"

"Look, I'm going to say what I think and there's nothing you can do about it. You said you wouldn't do these kinds of things anymore. You promised. Now you're acting like-"

"Thank you, Mr. Perfect!" Nico exclaimed angrily, cutting Lucien off before he could finish. "As if I need you to remind me of what I said. I've got this, okay? This has nothing to do with Marielle. I'm just looking and ain't no harm in that."

"Oh there's some harm in it, all right. This is wrong. Looking tends to get you into trouble, Nico, and you damn sure don't need any more of that. Besides, there's a storm coming. We should get out of here before it gets bad."

Nicodemus groaned, wishing that his brother would shut up so that he could concentrate on the beautiful woman. Lucien was right about one thing. She *did* bear a remarkable resemblance to Marielle, and he couldn't help but stare at her. Seeing her made him feel calmer and more relaxed. When she had walked past him, the sheer scent of the Magnolia blossom she wore in her hair had been enough to turn his head. And now that his head was turned, he intended to look for as long as he liked.

His mind flashed to Marielle sitting at her vanity. She would always softly sing "Strange Fruit," a song by Billie Holiday, as she strategically placed the white Magnolia blossom she always wore in her curly, black hair. The song was so sad and somber with so much regretful emotion regarding racism in the South that it could bring a person to tears; but it sounded strangely beautiful when Marielle sang it for some reason.

Southern trees bear a strange fruit

Blood on the leaves and blood at the root

Black bodies swinging in the Southern breeze

Strange fruit hanging from the Poplar Trees

Nico breathed in deeply, remembering the sweet sound of Marielle's voice singing as he stood watching the woman through the open shutters of an old house in the French Quarter. She hummed a little tune as she undressed slowly, letting her dress slip from her beautiful, statuesque body in dramatic fashion... the same way Marielle would do before she'd take her long bubble baths.

She had the same skin as Marielle... the same style. She had the same supple breasts and curvaceous hips. Even her vaginal area was covered in thick black hair which curled this way and that just like Marielle's... *au naturale.* God, she *was* Marielle! Maybe he hadn't killed her after all. Maybe she'd lived and just decided not to come home.

The gush of sentimental, almost love that he'd felt for Marielle after he'd ravaged her surged through his chest nostalgically and his eyes beamed with admiration and emotion.

"No, Nico, you can't! You've got that look in your eye. Listen to me! You know what happens when-"

"Shhhh! She'll hear you. Then she'll call the cops. I'm gonna be Senator, asshole, I can't go to jail for watching some woman bathe. How will that look," Nico scolded his brother. "Now be quiet!"

"Nico, don't you think that if you really plan on making our family proud and showing that you're worthy of our forgiveness that maybe we shouldn't be here? I mean, how will you ever prove yourself to *Maman* if-"

"*Maman?*"

Just the sound of her name sent a cold chill through his entire body. Nico's voice trailed off and his eyes glossed over. His heart began to thunder painfully in his chest as he thought of the tall, overbearing, linebacker built woman who was, unfortunately, his mother. He could see her stiff, linen, dress that scratched your skin when she passed by you. Then there was her coal, black, hair curled tightly to her head in coarse sprigs, too short to put on actual curlers so she always wore it tied up in a scarf. Of course her piercing, steel, grey eyes that could see straight into you and fleshy mouth twisted in that permanent angry scowl were still en tact just the way he remembered.

He felt his stomach curdle and spoil just thinking of her, as everything around him seemed to become blurry and fade to black. Within seconds, there he was again- a tall, gangly boy of 12 years with clumsy, knobby knees and ashy legs. He could see himself so clearly. His hands were bloody again. Those damned blossoms were floating on the water in that glass bowl again, and *Maman* was angry… *again*.

"Maman, no! Please! Don't! I won't do it again, I promise!"

Maman shook her head looking conflicted but resolved to do what was best. She wasn't going to fall for his pleading again.

"Shut up, you pup! You demonic little pup! You're evil! Look what you have done," she said pointing to the battered, unrecognizable body slumped over in the corner stinking in the summer heat.

The skull was badly crushed, with gooey, grey, brain matter and blood leaking out to make a mushy soup on the floor; and there were a few giant flies crawling over the space where the eyes should have been.

"I'm sorry, Maman! It was an accident. I'm a good boy! I brought you Magnolias this morning! Fresh! Just like you like 'em! Please don't hurt me! I didn't mean to do The Bad Thing again!"

Maman paced the floor wringing her hands nervously, unsure of what to do with her son. She shook her head, ready to break down into tears, but knew she had to be strong. She had to do God's work. There was no other choice. She'd been given Nicodemus for a son for a reason. God wanted her to be His vessel. He wanted her to lead the way in the fight against evil, and she had to have faith in His plan if she were going to do so. If Abraham could follow God's orders to sacrifice Isaac who was good, she was certain that she could sacrifice Nicodemus who was evil.

"Take off all your clothes, Nicodemus! Do it now!"

Nico felt his chest heaving up and down. What would she do to him now? His trembling fingers, smeared with blood that wasn't even his own, removed his shirt and exposed his blue, black, and purple back, bruised cruelly from previous beatings.

"Take off everything!"

"But you'll see my privates! You'll see it and try to touch it like Father Mereaux does! I don't like when he touches me!"

"Blasphemer! You will burn in the fiery pits of hell in eternal darkness for your lies! There is no purer soul on this Earth than Father Mereaux, you filfthy heathen and I will not let you taint his good name! Now, take your clothes off! Don't make me tell you again!"

Filled with apprehension and dread, he unbuttoned his patched corduroy pants and slipped them off, then peeled off his dingy, yellowed underwear that were once white. He stood there, naked and sweaty, feeling ashamed in front of his mother.

He was a boy of twelve with his bruised and battered, hairless body and limp penis completely exposed. If only he could stop doing The Bad Thing, he wouldn't have to endure the beatings or the humiliation. And he certainly didn't want to have to go to the church to repent with Father Mereaux where he'd have his penis stroked during confession. That was his punishment for being bad. Father Mereaux called it releasing the demons.

"I knew the first time I held you as a baby I should have given you back to the good Lord right off the bat. Maybe it would have saved your soul and poor Lucien's too. But no, I fell victim to the weakness of love. I loved you and kept you with me, damning your soul forever. I thought I could save you, Nicodemus, but I was wrong. There is no salvation for you. Nothing can save you now. Nothing!"

She swung the wooden broom with all of her might, cracking Nico across his bare back with it. He fell over, stunned by the sudden blow that took his breath away and knocked the bowl full of water and blossoms down to the floor with him. Water, shards of glass, and white Magnolias splattered everywhere filling the room with the creamy scent of lemon, vanilla, and honeysuckle in contrast to the metallic, bodily odor of spilled blood.

Terrified of what his mother would do next, Nico covered his head with his bloody hands, praying she would stop. But there was nothing that could have stopped her, she was too angry. He had done The Bad Thing again and had to be punished. That was the way of things.

She brought the broom down in hard, swift blows, beating the boy mercilessly across his body until he could barely move. Each blow sounded with a sickening thud against his body, creating new clots of bruised blood beneath his sweaty, brown skin. He could hear the broom sailing through the air with a sharp whistle as it landed with full force each time. He curled himself into a ball, as hot, hysterical tears streamed out of his eyes. His body shook uncontrollably, unable to stop.

Lucien stood off away from his mother and brother watching unemotionally.

"It'll be over soon," he mouthed silently to Nico as he stared straight ahead blankly.

"You devil! You spawn! You disgrace! You will bring shame to us all! Your father should have killed you at birth, God rest his weary soul!"

Maman kicked her heavy foot out and caught Nico in his ribs. He shrieked like an inhuman creature from the blinding pain, barely able to maintain his consciousness. His mother crossed herself.

"Lord, please forgive me for allowing this filth to continue breathing, but I haven't the strength to kill my own child! I love him! God help me, but I do!"

She brought the broom down in one final crack across the side of his head splitting it open like a melon. Blood oozed down his face and into his eyes, mixing with the sweat and dust on the floor of their little shack. Still he was relieved that the beating had finally stopped- at least he was still alive even if only barely. He lingered there in a state of semi-consciousness, waiting for the pain to cause him to black out like it always did.

Maman looked down at him, her huge body trembling with blind rage as she crossed herself again.

"The Lord put me on this earth to smite Evil, and damn it that's what I'm gonna do!"

Maman grabbed Nico's leg. God's work wasn't done just yet. Her son would have to repent before it was all said and done.

"Maman, pleasssse, noooo. Pleasssse don'tttt," Nico whimpered, his words slurring thanks to the new unnatural angle of his jaw.

His mother didn't seem to notice or care that he was bloodied and bruised. She dragged him across the wooden floor, digging splinters deep into his bare skin.

She drug him down the jagged, wooden steps, not caring that his head crashed on each one, splattering wet, red blood all over them from his oozing gash. She drug him, cruelly, through the grainy dirt and across itchy, green grass... across coarse tree roots and over fire-ant hills through the yard.

When she'd finally gotten him far out into the yard away from the house, Nico was barely conscious. His naked body was covered in scrapes, cuts, bruises, and nasty gouges. His eyes had rolled up into the back of his head, showing the whites and his breathing was extremely shallow.

"Pray that death finds you here, Nicodemus. Please know that I do love you. I love you so much. You're my eldest child, but your soul needs to be released. You belong with the Lord. He can do more for you than I could ever do. Take him, Lord!"

Maman closed her eyes and sighed, then took her foot and regretfully pushed her son down into the old, shallow well. Nico's body hit the waist high water with a huge splash as his face scraped against the stone walls. His eyes, clouded over with blood, looked up blurrily towards his mother, who had fallen down to her knees with her hands clasped in prayer. Rosary beads were intertwined in her fingers as she prayed for forgiveness. It wasn't the first time she'd kicked him down the well, but this was the first time she'd ever beaten him quite so brutally. Oh there were plenty of other beatings to be sure, but never this bad. Maybe The Bad Thing was Really Bad this time.

"Maman, pleasssse help meeee," he strained. "I'm sorrrry. Pleasssseeee. I- I repent!"

Tears streaked down Maman's face, wanting so desperately to believe him. But it was a trick. She knew it. He'd say anything to get himself out of the well. Her son was evil and the only way he'd ever fully repent was to send his soul on to glory.

"Go in peace, Nicodemus. Go in peace. God will take care of you. And if the Good Lord won't have you and keep you, Father Mereaux will make you repent somehow. Father Mereaux will make you release your demons over and over again. Forgive me, Father!"

"Mamannnn!"

The vision faded to black as Nico's body shivered and shuddered from the distant echo of his screams. His eyes rolled around in his head looking like cue balls.

"Nicodemus! Snap out of it and look at this mess!"

Nico gasped, as he felt his head throbbing. His blood was racing so fast that he could hear it rushing feverishly past his ears. When he finally looked down, his heart jumped in his throat and adrenaline flooded his senses. His hands were dripping in thick, chunky, red blood and one hand gripped a butcher knife.

"What the fuck!" he screamed.

He dropped the knife to the floor, stumbling away from the body of the naked woman who had been stabbed so many times that her flesh looked like pig slop. Blood was everywhere. The once light blue carpet of the house was now a deep, dark, burgundy. The white Magnolia blossom that had been in her hair- the thing that had probably sealed her fate, was now stained a deep crimson as it lie in a pool of blood.

"What did I do? What the fuck did I just do?" Nico exclaimed, trembling.

"You did *it* again, that's what you did. You did The Bad Thing. I'm so tired of this, Nico. Don't you think I get tired of cleaning up your messes? Seriously, were you born attached at the hip with that knife or what," Lucien exclaimed, shaking his head. "Primitive ass knife… Try a gun next time! At least it's cleaner and I won't be stuck down here on my hands and knees scrubbing body chunks out of the carpet!"

Nico looked down at the woman who had looked so much like Marielle before, but now looked like someone else entirely- at least from what he could make out of her mangled face. She didn't resemble Marielle in the least bit with the exception of that damn flower. It was the visions… they'd gotten him again- tricked him again. Tricked him into killing…

"I can fix this," Nico said taking a deep breath and clearing his throat. "This is no problem. I can fix this one."

"I sure would pay big money to see *that* happen," Lucien replied rolling his eyes.

"No, I can fix this, I really can. I can make everything alright again. This doesn't mean anything, Lucien. All we need is a little bleach and no one will ever know we were here."

"Oh just a little bleach, huh? That'll do the trick? You really *are* delusional. This is sick, Nico. I think it's time you admit you have a problem. I'm not so sure Dr. Thibideaux ever really helped you at all. To think you spent all those years in that room talking to him about your problems only to get nothing out of it."

Lucien sighed dramatically and threw up his hands.

"Maybe Father Mereaux really *is* the only person that can help, just like *Maman* said."

Nico felt the vein in his temples pulse as hot anger pumped into his blood.

"DON'T YOU EVER TALK ABOUT FATHER MEREAUX TO ME OR I'LL SLIT YOUR FUCKING THROAT! DO YOU UNDERSTAND ME?"

Lucien sighed again and rolled his eyes to the ceiling.

"You're such a drama king, you know that? That was always your problem. Always wearing your emotions on your sleeve like a little ass girl, going off, whining, and crying."

"Shut up!"

"Didn't get picked for football, cry like a little bitch," Lucien continued tauntingly relaying memories from their childhood. "*Maman* whooped your ass for killing innocent girls, you cry like a little bitch. Now, if I mention Father Mereaux, you still cry like a little bitch! Ugh! When are you going to grow some balls and own up to the shit that you did and stop all the crying and whining?"

"Shut up! Just shut up! You're trying to hurt me, but you can't because I'm past all that now, Lucien! I've grown!"

Lucien rolled his eyes again unconvinced.

"Whatever. We still have a damn big problem on our hands here, Nico with this dead body. Am I allowed to talk about *that*?"

Nico shook his head pacing back and forth as his stomach churned and curdled. He could feel his ass ready to let loose another load of watery shit. He began to beat the sides of his head with his fists, pacing faster and faster.

"Look, we don't have time for this nonsense. You need to suck it up. We've gotta clean up this evidence before someone figures out that we've been here. Have you forgotten you've just committed a murder?"

Nico ignored his brother and focused on the feelings of guilt taking over his body.

"Oh no, not happening! Not fuckin' happening!" Nico cried out, beating his head and whimpering to himself.

"Pull yourself together, man! We gotta get out of here before the storm hits! I can smell the rain coming. You do realize that if the storm catches us here, we'll probably be arrested for murder and thrown in a cell with some big, sloppy Swamp Man named Bubba, right?"

Nico didn't reply. He just stared at the body, pacing back and forth and beating the sides of his head muttering to himself.

"I just can't believe you've dragged me into the middle of one of your crazy fits yet again. I'm done with your ass for good this time."

Nico continued pacing and muttering inaudible words. Lucien's face clouded with anger.

"Nigga, do you hear me talking to you?! Focus! You're so fuckin' selfish! You never care what mess you get others into! All you care about is yourself! If we get caught, it's not just your ass on the line here, it's mine too!"

"I'm sorry, Lucien. I really didn't mean it. I just thought she looked so much like Marielle. Even you thought so."

"You moron, Marielle is dead! You killed her. This woman looks nothing like Mari," Lucien replied nastily. "Why did you even follow her? I told you that this was nothing but trouble! But as usual, you think you know everything and landed us in deep shit yet again!"

"But you agreed, Lucien! You agreed that she looked like Marielle! I heard you! You told me she was beautiful! Admit it!"

Suddenly Nico could hear a soft and delicate voice singing. It had to be the most beautiful sound he'd ever heard. It was the song he had heard her singing so often before, as she combed her beautiful, black hair.

"Southern trees bear a strange fruit..."

Nico gasped.

"You hear that?"

Lucien busied himself with the bleach, scrubbing the objects in the house that he and Nico had touched.

"Get your mind in the game, Nico, if you ever want the chance to be Senator and do what you promised to do for this family. Help me clean this mess up. Get the knife and clean it. I'm not cleaning this up by myself!"

"Blood on the leaves, and blood at the roots. Black bodies swinging…"

"It's her… she's here."

"Who? Who's here? Get the knife! We might have to kill them too! We can't leave any witnesses!"

"No! It's Mari! She's here. I hear her. Don't you hear the song, Lucien? It's *her* song."

Nicodemus looked at Lucien with bright hope in his eyes. Lucien shook his head disapprovingly.

"You're losing it, Nico. Seriously. There's nobody there. Nobody is singing. But I'll tell you what *is* here. There *is* a whole lot of blood on the floor. You wanna focus on that?"

Nico looked frantically all around him, hearing the song in every direction.

"She's everywhere. She came for me. I can feel her essence."

He stepped over the naked woman's body, not giving a damn that he had blood all over his clothes and hands.

"I don't care what you say, Lucien. I hear her. I hear Marielle. What does she want? Do you think she's angry? I made love to her, Lucien. I made love to her before she died in the hospital and it was so beautiful. I really think we had a connection," Nico declared as he lovingly closed his eyes in sweet remembrance.

   "... *in the Southern breeze... Strange fruit hanging from the Poplar Trees...*"

Suddenly Nico's stomach growled violently making Nico's eyes pop open like a wild man's.

"You better not do it!" Lucien warned. "You better control it this time!"

"*Ahnnnnh,*" Nico groaned in intense pain. "It hurts so badddd!"

He couldn't hold it anymore. He doubled over, slipping on all the blood on the floor as his pants filled with nasty fecal matter again, running down his legs. Lucien sighed knowing it was only a matter of time before his brother shit himself.

"Now how did I know that was coming," he asked himself sarcastically. "Nico, I love you man, I really do but is there anything about me that says janitor to you? I might help you with cleaning up this blood and hiding this body, but you're for damn sure going to wipe your own ass and clean up your own shit! You ain't a baby and I'm no nanny. I don't change diapers. Now get up before we get caught! Didn't I tell you a storm was coming? You're such a disgrace! And a shitty one at that!"

Nico covered his ears with his bloody hands trying to block out Lucien's words. He could feel the fear and anger bubbling inside him, opening his bowels more and more. A steady brown stream spilled down his leg filling the room with the smell of burning rubber and something long dead.

"I won't listen! I won't listen to you, Lucien! You just want to hurt me! I won't listen!"

"You're such a disgrace, Nico! A disgrace! *Maman* was right! Do you hear me! You've disgraced this family!"

The words echoed over and over in Nico's head in long winding syllables.

"No!" he screamed as he beat the sides of his head with his fists. "No, please! I'm a good boy! *Maman*, I'm so sorry! Don't beat me! Don't throw me down the well!"

CHAPTER VII

Aleera had avoided Charlize for the rest of the day. Something about her words just didn't sit well. *Madame Blanchard will have her revenge, make no mistake about that...* It left a bad taste in her mouth. Aleera considered herself a thorough chick, not really ghetto, but she'd bust somebody's ass if the occasion called for it. She certainly wasn't one to let any broad scare her or talk shit to her, but something about the way Charlize had said those creepy words made her feel nervous. Not that she was scared or anything. She just didn't need Charlize sticking a voodoo doll with pins or performing some headless chicken ceremony with strands of her weave.

Determined to stay away from Charlize while the storm raged outside, Aleera headed upstairs to explore the great mansion. It had become a new favorite pastime of hers. After all, there was so much to see in the old house.

The beautiful, antebellum, main house had 25 grandeur rooms in total. All of the rooms were lavish and luxurious as could be expected in a mansion like Blanchard Manor. And out of all the 25 rooms which included 6 bedrooms, there was one room in particular that Aleera just couldn't seem to keep herself away from. Of course, it had to be the room of her lover's dead wife- a woman with whom she had grown strangely obsessed since living in the house.

Nico had demanded that she stay out of there for whatever reason. He'd been chomping at the bit like a rabid Pit Bull when she had asked him about it, growing so enraged at the mere mention of Marielle that for a moment, Aleera couldn't help but wonder who the hell she was sitting there talking to: Nico or Cujo? To calm him down, or at least get him to stop yelling and looking so damn crazy, she had agreed to stay out of there. But in the end, she just couldn't do it. Besides, why should she? She was entitled to see what that stuck up bitch had in her room.

Like the prissy, little princess she was, Marielle had had the grandest bedroom in the house. It was called The Swan Room and for good reason. In the middle of the room on a grand platform, was an ornate, gilded swan bed draped in heavy silk dressing. The gold headboard had an embroidered, cursive M and B intertwined, which obviously stood for *Marielle Blanchard*. Around it was a pale, pink, sheer draping that encased the bed in a beautiful canopy. To say that it was regal would have been an understatement. That bed had been specially crafted for a goddess.

The room was huge even by mansion standards. There were beautiful sofas upholstered in the same heavy silk as the bed dressing. In front of them was a carved Cherry wood, coffee table topped with polished marble. The center piece was a large, glass vase filled with water, with Magnolia blossoms floating on the surface. All of this was positioned cozily in front of the ornately carved, Italian marble mantel.

Above the mantel, there was a huge portrait of Marielle dressed in a gorgeous, rose colored gown. The gown was late 1700s French style- attire befitting a Queen. And though the portrait captured Marielle's legendary power, class, and beauty, it also managed to capture a bit of innocence with the white Magnolia blossom that adorned her hair.

This bitch really thought she was something special didn't she, Aleera wondered to herself jealously as the pit of her stomach churned with hatred for a woman she'd never met. She rolled her eyes, feeling herself want to puke all over Marielle's fancy floor as she took a sip of vodka.

The hatred stabbed at her so badly, that she felt like the air in that room, thick with Marielle's essence was almost choking her. It was almost like Marielle's spirit still lurked in each of her possessions repelling Aleera like garlic repels a vampire.

Still, in some strange way, though she was sickened by all the adoration that the spoiled little princess seemed to have in life, Aleera still found that she was eerily drawn to her things and the thought of Marielle, herself, like a moth to a flame. She was beginning to wonder if she really *was* obsessed with the woman.

Aleera shivered as she listened to the grumbling thunder outside and stared at the mesmerizing portrait. She stood there for nearly 15 minutes with her mouth hanging open and her eyes narrowed to jealous slits. She gulped down the rest of her liquor and let out a disgusting burp, then slammed her glass on the marble coffee table. She was tired of looking at Marielle even though the portrait seemed to compel her to stare at it. Still, she wanted to see the rest of the room so she tore herself from it and staggered away from the picture.

There were French, double doors near the bed that led out to a private terrace with sheer draping, giving it an open summertime feel. But the thing that caught Aleera's attention the most (other than that portrait which had served to induce her gag reflex) was the huge walk in closet located on the opposite side of the room from the bed.

She wobbled towards it wide eyed, knowing that a rich little Creole girl like Marielle would have been spoiled with beautiful gowns and dresses made from the finest imported fabrics by a plethora of French and Italian designers. Aleera would bet money that *De La Renta's* entire spring line was probably hanging up in that gigantic closet with no owner to show it off.

She opened the doors excitedly ready to possess everything a closet like that could yield. And just as she'd expected, the closet more than delivered. There were shelves upon shelves of pumps, boots, sandals, and flats by every funny named designer you could think of. There were boxes upon boxes of *Hermes* purses neatly placed on shelves, looking as though they'd just been flown in from Paris. Each shelf housed its own miniature chandelier to light the extensive closet. And the clothes, of course, were a gold digger's paradise.

There were haute couture gowns by designers that Aleera had never even heard of, and even Marielle's everyday clothes could rival the Royal Family's.

"Prissy little bitch," she slurred to herself feeling sick just thinking of Marielle prancing around in the gowns. "Everything going to waste. I bet some of this shit would look good on me, though."

Aleera grabbed a white, one shouldered, flowing gown from the many luxurious dresses. It struck a chord in her soul, somehow. Her eyes grew huge and glossy just looking at it. It really seemed to call her name- to whisper softly to her in her ear. She instinctively measured it against her body with her eyes as big and bright as diamonds, completely mesmerized by the dress that wasn't hers but should have been.

"Doubt you'll be needing this anymore, boo! Can't take it with ya," she exclaimed excitedly.

Aleera took off her clothes quickly, and slid the dress off the hanger. What good were all those clothes going to do anybody hanging up all lonely in that closet? It wasn't like their owner was coming back to claim them. Once you're dead and gone, you're dead and gone. No exceptions.

She slid the dress on, wiggling, sucking herself in, and pulling to get it on. Aleera was a lot thicker than Marielle, so the fabric clung to her curves like saran wrap. The gown was made to flow effortlessly but it looked like a tight, spandex dress on Aleera. Her plump, store bought, round ass and curvaceous hips gave it a look that passed sexy and made a right turn at slutty. Her big, silicone titties didn't do it much justice either. They bulged from the top of the dress, damn near ready to pop. But you couldn't tell Aleera that she didn't look damn good in that dress. In her mind, that dress was made for her. She didn't know why, but as soon as she'd pulled it on, she'd instantly felt that she was entitled to that dress. It was *hers*.

She swayed drunkenly out of the closet feeling amazing- feeling majestic but looking more like a pissy stripper than a goddess. This was *her* room. She laid herself across the Swan Bed and sighed pleasurably, feeling orgasmic.

"I could get used to this. All of this should be mine."

She thought of how good she'd look as the lady of Nico's house. She'd be in Socialite heaven if he married her. She thought of all the parties, and people flashing their cameras to take pictures of her- the new Lady of Blanchard Manor. Maybe they'd even rename the estate. Maybe it would be LaCroix Manor, home of Lord and Lady LaCroix. *Lady LaCroix...*

The thought of renewed fame and fortune washed over her like warm sunlight. That *would* be divine. She'd been waiting to get back into the limelight for a very long time, but never once thought she'd have a shot at being a woman of New Orleans Society Life. Hell, maybe they'd even give her a spread in *Home and Garden* magazine! Only the rich of the rich make in there! The thoughts tickled her pink and she giggled girlishly, kicking her legs with excitement.

Creak...

Aleera suddenly sat up, her thoughts interrupted by a deliberate, low, creaking. Almost as if someone had stepped on a loose floorboard.

She looked around the beautiful room, eyeing every nook and cranny. Nothing had changed. Everything looked as perfectly blurry as it always did in her drunken haze. Everything except the shadows in the corners that seemed to be growing and the lights that seemed to be flickering. And of course there was also the growing, chilling cold that forced her to shiver against her will. The hairs on the back of neck stood up and goose flesh pimpled her arms.

Then the low creaking came again, only now it was becoming a long, pronounced whine- an old house groaning from the pressure of *something*.

"Is anyone there?" she called out, immediately feeling stupid as if whoever was there, if there were anyone there at all, would actually answer her. But she did have the feeling that someone was watching her… watching her and hating her.

Abruptly, the French doors to the terrace flew open with the force of an explosion as the fabric draping began flapping angrily in the strong wind that suddenly beat the house mercilessly. Aleera screamed out, terrified.

She could feel her heart beating 1000 times a minute and the blood flowing in her veins turned to ice. She eased herself from the bed, and crept slowly, cautiously to the doors to shut them and find whatever had forced them open that way. Suddenly messing around in Marielle's room didn't seem like such a good idea. Still, she was no punk and she wasn't going to let something as stupid as the doors being blown open frighten her.

She could hear the wind howling outside like a lost lover and the sudden pouring of rain. The lights flickered a bit making the light bulbs hum and the walls of the house seemed to groan in pain. Her chest rose and fell dramatically, and her mouth had gone dry and sour from a sudden, cold fear.

She slowly eased herself onto her tippy toes to peek out on the terrace, terrified of what she might find. She could feel her hands trembling from the panic that was rising inside of her and the feeling of eyes watching her was growing by the second. Suddenly her nose filled with a dreadful, rotten stench so horrible that she felt her stomach lurching to vomit. She retched.

"I thought I told you never to come in here," said a low creepy voice dripping with cruel intentions.

Aleera whipped around so fast she was sure she had whiplash. Nico was standing there staring at her with black eyes- eyes she'd never seen before. She hadn't even heard him come in. His hands were bloody and so were his clothes. His shoes were smudged in dark mud (or was that shit), and his presence loomed dangerously.

"N- Nico, baby! Wh- what happened to you? Are you alright?" The words caught in her throat.

The room seemed to fill with the smell of rotten feces immediately, as if the smell, itself, had been waiting for the right time to devour the fresh air.

Aleera instantly felt like prey in the crosshairs of a murderous hunter with the way that Nico was staring at her. His expression was demented and his eyes were empty. He looked like Nico, but it certainly didn't *feel* like Nico. No… Aleera strangely felt that somehow, and she couldn't possibly explain how, but somehow the man standing there who looked exactly like her lover was something else- something evil.

He licked his lips hungrily. It reminded Aleera of a serpent.

"B-baby?" she asked frightened.

"You have no idea, do you? You look so much like her. So much! You look like…"

His voice trailed off distantly and his eyes seemed to gloss over like his thoughts were a million miles away. He walked over to the coffee table and picked a fresh, floating, Magnolia blossom from the centerpiece sitting there. His bloodied, shitty fingers smudged the white blossom a disgusting mixture of red and brown. Smiling evilly, he placed the blossom in Aleera's black and royal blue streaked weave.

"There. Now you look like her. Beautiful. Like an angel. She was my angel. Did you know that? She was everybody's angel."

Aleera wrinkled up her face in anger and smacked the Magnolia out of her weave. *What the hell was going on? Who was his damn angel?*

"What the fuck are you doing, Nico?"

"No, you wouldn't know that she was my angel, would you? You couldn't know that. I didn't tell you. But she was. My angel- my beautiful Marielle. And now you look just like her. Just like my angel."

"Oh I know you're not comparing me to that stuck up bitch! And where the hell are you coming from smelling like a sewer and looking like you done shot somebody? Oh, so all of a sudden you 'bout that life?"

"Simply beautiful…"

"Nigga, I ain't trying to hear that bullshit! I asked you where the hell you're coming from?!"

Nico's face crumbled and morphed into a mask of intense, fiery anger. His eyes went as dark as the night. There was no love in them… no recognition… no soul.

"You bitch! You fuckin' bitch! I should have never married you! You're always judging me! Do you think you're better? Huh? Do you? Answer me!"

"What? What are you talking-"

"I'm the man in this house! Not you! Do you hear me you filthy whore! You'll do what I say! You'll do what I tell you!"

"N- Nico! What the hell-"

Nico didn't let her get another word out of her mouth. He slapped her across the face so hard that she fell backwards onto the Swan Bed. He roared like a vicious monster.

No, Nico, don't hurt her!

He ignored the distant voice of his brother and continued to rage. He climbed on top of Aleera. *This is what the fuck she deserves for looking like Marielle! For coming into Marielle's room when he'd demanded that she stay out!* He smacked her again, bruising her jaw and forced her arms over her head.

"What are you doing? Have you lost your mind! What the fuck are you doing? Nico! Stop!"

Nico ripped through the delicate fabric of the now, stained dress, exposing Aleera's naked body. He was hard… too hard. Too hard not to take her right there on Marielle's bed. She was wearing the dress he'd given Marielle to wear on their wedding anniversary. The white, flowing, virginal dress that looked so beautiful on her. Now, it was stained with Aleera's body in it… now it was tainted. He'd have to punish her. This was Marielle's room- *her* pure, virginal room. Aleera was a whore. She didn't belong in it. He'd teach her. He'd teach her what happens when she disobeyed.

His penis was so hard that the veins crisscrossed his shaft and bulged outwards like tree roots. And without a word of warning or preparation, he forced himself inside Aleera, pushing her panties inside of her right along with him. She screamed in agony, as his penis seemed to burn her flesh while he sawed her in half, pumping, impaling, and huffing.

"Nico, stop! Stop! Please! You're hurting me! Get the fuck off of me!"

But he didn't stop. He couldn't. The sound of his skin smacking up against hers made him feel powerful- invincible even. The pain in her eyes was perfect and he could barely hold himself together when the tears streaked down her cheeks in black, smudgy streams from her running mascara. He pumped harder, and held her in place by her neck.

He was beginning to feel it- that liquid God invoking feeling that would swallow any man into a vortex of deliciousness. It was getting ready to come spewing out in one big volcanic rush. He needed to look in her eyes while it happened. He forced her head still so that he could look deeply at her… but her face was no longer hers. Her weave was gone and in its place was Marielle's black hair laying in curled masses with that signature white blossom. Aleera's dark brown eyes were gone and in its place were Marielle's hazel eyes. Her mouth was smiling at him seductively- invitingly; smiling the way that she'd never smiled at him in life.

"Give it to me, Nicodemus. Give it to me hard! Cum inside me! Give me the child we never had!"

His entire ten year marriage, he had longed for Marielle to say those words to him. She was so conservative that the only time they had had sex without a condom was when she was in the hospital right before her... death. She could sense the insanity within him-could sense that he was disturbed. As a result, she only let him touch her once a day. That was why he'd needed Aleera. But now... now after all these years, she was finally ready to let him have her completely of her own free will. Finally she had come to her senses. All he'd had to do was kill her. His heart thundered in his chest with excitement

"Are you sure, *ma cherie*? Are you sure you want my son," he whispered breathlessly. "I can give him to you. Just let me know."

"Nico, let me go! Please! You're hurting me!" Aleera screamed, her throat raw. "What's the matter with you? Are you fuckin' nuts? You're tearing my insides! Let me go or I'll call the cops!"

Those words seemed to fall on deaf ears. Nico couldn't see or hear Aleera at all. All he saw was Marielle's beautiful face, lying on her beautiful, Swan Bed, in her beautiful, white, virginal gown. He looked at her adoringly, wanting nothing more than to climax inside his beloved.

"Yes my love, give me your son. I love you. I want you. I forgive you. Cum inside me."

"Beg me! Beg me to do it!" he exclaimed feeling himself grow more and more excited as he continued thrashing Aleera.

"Please stop, Nico! Please! I *am* begging you! Please! Stop!"

"Please cum inside me, baby! Give me all your creamy, white glaze! I want it inside me, now! I want your baby!"

"Ohhhh Mariiii! Ohhhh Mariii! I can't hold itttt!" Nico exclaimed as he came inside of Aleera in static, repetitious spurts.

He trembled with pleasure and sighed as he collapsed, sweaty, on Aleera's body, his hands pressed up against her cheeks which were now smudged with make-up and shit. Aleera cried out softly, never experiencing anything so heinous and horrible in her life and she shook violently with shock and shame.

Nico looked down, satisfied, ready to finally tell his wife how much he cared for her. He blinked, confused and felt a pang in his chest, suddenly frightened. He swallowed, feeling out of breath.

"Wh- What are you doing here, Lee? Where is she," he swallowed. "Where's Marielle?"

Aleera didn't bother answering. All she could do was focus on the pain throbbing between her legs and the horrendous smell that seemed to invade her nose. She turned her head to the side, not wanting to look at him, and whimpered from the pain and the shame.

Then came the laughter, vibrating through the air. Distant, barely audible, maniacal laughter seemingly coming from nowhere at all… She couldn't hear it… not in her ears, but she could sense it in her head and she could feel it vibrate through her body.

The laughter came from the room. It came from every shadow and every corner. It came from the thunder roaring outside, and the rain hissing from the downpour. It came from the wind howling in the night and the weeping willow trees bending from the violence of the thunderstorm. But most of all, it came from that horrible portrait that looked down at them, watching as Nico savagely raped her.

It was the room. It was *her* room. Somehow, it was the room all along. The abuse, the rape, everything… *It was that got damned room…*

CHAPTER VIII

Aleera sat up suddenly and looked all around the room, feeling like she could bawl her eyes out from the abuse and rape Nico had just done to her, but she gasped in shock! Everything was different! Nico wasn't there at all. Nothing in the room had changed. In fact, she still had on her own clothes. Marielle's white dress was nowhere to be found.

She looked down and saw the glass of vodka she'd been drinking shattered on the floor. She'd dropped it. Her cell phone was sitting on the little couch in front of the marble coffee table. She'd been laying there and fallen asleep. *It was a dream! It was a gotdamn dream!*

The realization and relief washed over her in a tsunami wave. Why in the world would she have dreamt something so horrible? She rubbed her mouth and lips with the back of her hand- a clear indication that she needed another drink. *Damn it*, all that drinking had finally driven her insane. Now the craving for more was literally making her body ache. She suddenly felt sick.

"I gotta get control of this shit," she said to herself out loud. "All this damn drinking is really starting to fuck me up. I swore I wouldn't let this shit control my life."

She took a deep breath and ran her hands down her face, wanting another drink more than ever. God, she hadn't felt cravings like this in years. Sure she'd been hitting the bottle a lot more lately and popping a few pills, but never had her body seemed so forceful in wanting it. She looked up at the looming picture of Marielle and gasped. It seemed to be smiling at her where it definitely didn't have a smile before. And that smile, staring down at her in some mocking way, seemed to make the cravings within Aleera stronger than ever.

"Unnnnnnh," she groaned, feeling almost as if she would vomit.

She needed something to help her right away or there was going to be a new art form on Marielle's fancy floor. Maybe if she took a bath, she could sweat it out. She held her stomach and staggered into Marielle's bathroom feeling wobbly and unsteady on her feet. Something was wrong. She was beginning to feel like she didn't have control over herself anymore. The dream had been too real. And though it was obviously a dream, it felt like *something* had actually happened in there- something other than the rape and the abuse in her head. In her dream, it was like it wasn't Nico doing all those horrific things to her- not in his eyes. Looking into his eyes had been like looking into a dark abyss of smoldering evil... the Devil's eyes. That thing raping her wasn't Nico. It was something else.

She could feel it- the blackness of it all. It was prickly, empty, and cold- unnaturally cold like toes nipped with frost bite. And it was hollow, like the black uncertainty that lies in a deserted grave. It wrapped around her like a coiled snake, squeezing her tight, and slithering up and down her body. Ever since she'd stepped foot in that room, she could feel traces of it. But she'd been so blinded by its beauty and the unbelievable way that Marielle had obviously been spoiled, that she looked past that creeping feeling. Had looked past that bitter blackness and shrugged it off in order to reap the benefits. After all, Marielle was dead. What harm could it do?

Madame Blanchard will have her revenge, make no mistake about that...

Charlize's words echoed in her ears and made her shudder. Is that what that beastly, polluted feeling was that crept down her spine and settled into her bones? Marielle's revenge?

In the dream, when Nico had hit her and even worse, had raped her, that evil seemed to intensify. It seemed to grow colder and blacker than ever. It spilled over into the air of the room like a bubbling, putrefied poison. And it possessed Nico, morphing him into some wretched form of himself.

Still, it was just a dream. That was it. No matter how real it felt, the truth was that she'd been asleep and thought it all up in her head. So why did she feel so afraid now that she was awake? Why was her body so traumatized that it craved alcohol like a baby craves its mother's milk? That room was doing it. Somehow, and she didn't know how, but that room was making it all happen. And yet strangely, she couldn't bring herself to leave it just yet.

Aleera sighed wearily and filled the huge, claw-foot tub, sitting in the middle of the beige and gold marble floor, with hot, soapy water. Maybe if she could soak her body in Marielle's pristine tub, she would be able to wash away the overwhelming, shadowy evil that seemed to coat her body like a putrid, second skin. She slipped down into the steamy, hot water and hung her head back to relax. It felt good... safe... comforting as her breasts floated like big buoys in the water.

And then it began again. That slow, deliberate, creaking... It seemed to ease its way into the bathroom, groaning as if the marble floor had somehow begun to breathe. Aleera's eyes immediately popped open, wide and alert with fear. *Not again...* She pinched her arm. It hurt... this time it wasn't a dream. This time she was wide awake.

"Is someone there?" she called out, looking all around the bathroom, feeling the fight or flight adrenaline pump like heroin through her veins. "Nico? Charlize?"

There was nothing. There was only the wet sound of water dripping from the faucet and rippling as it hit the soapy bathwater. Everything else looked the same. She exhaled, feeling her heart thumping in her chest.

"This place is fuckin' creepy," she said to herself aloud as she leaned her head back against the tub to relax again. "Rooms and shit making noises on their own... I'm losing it."

She took a deep breath and closed her eyes, but only for a moment. Marielle's room would give her no peace. The water in the claw-foot tub began to bubble around her rapidly, churning almost as if it were boiling. Her breath caught in her throat as she felt jittery panic creep up her legs, spill over into her stomach like dancing, white lightning, and continue up her arms.

"It's nothing," she whispered to herself sharply, her strained voice trembling. "It's nothing at all."

She clamped her eyes closed. It wasn't real. It couldn't be. She was dreaming. That's what it was. Another dream.

"I don't believe," she whispered, unable to keep her hands from shaking. "I *won't* believe."

The soapy water churned more and more, making it so hot in the huge bathroom that the mirrors fogged from the white steam. Aleera, too afraid to move, opened her eyes and stared at it, feeling a piercing, damnable, presence watching her again. She could feel its eyes searching her naked body, taking in every contour of it.

Slowly, an invisible finger, making that eerie, wet sound that only a finger on a wet surface can make, traced the words Y-O-U- W-I-L-L- D-I-E on the lighted mirror.

Aleera gasped as her internal temperature instantly plummeted to ten below zero despite the piping hot water. The hair on the back of her neck stood on end and her throat felt dry and cracked from bitter fear. A vicious scream raged behind her lips, but it was so intense that neither her tongue nor her lips would move.

The words dripped down into smeared lines as the condensation on the mirror began to run. Suddenly, an arm shot up out of the tub, grabbed Aleera by the weave, and pulled her underneath the soapy water! Horror throbbed through Aleera's body like a jolt of frozen electricity as she thrashed around like a wounded animal, fighting nothing to get out of the tub before it drowned her.

"Helpppp meeee!" she shrieked from the depths of her throat, as she managed to pop back up for air. "Nicoooo! Nicoooo, helpppp!"

She held on to the sides of the tub with all her might, struggling to stay above water as the black Evil clawed at her body like an animal, determined to throw her under again. She suddenly felt streaks of fire running up and down her legs and lower back. Deep cuts in her skin oozed blood as The Evil dug its razor sharp talons into her flesh.

"Let me goooo! Nicoooo!"

A flash in the mirror caught her eye, as she caught a quick glimpse of Marielle's smiling face... that same knowing, authoritative smile from the portrait above the mantel. Aleera's heart jumped in her throat and her flesh crawled as she fell backward from terror.

"Noooo! Oh my God, noooo!"

"Will *Madame* kindly stop screaming like a banshee? This is a respectable house. And you're getting water all over the floor, thrashing like a hippo. Are you having a seizure or something?"

Aleera looked up with a sharp gasp to see Charlize standing in the doorway with her hand on her hip and an indignant look on her face. Coming to her senses, Aleera looked frantically back at the mirror, making that huh-huh-huh sound, as she breathed heavily from fear.

Marielle's face was gone. So were those horrible words. The black Evil had miraculously dissipated into nothing. She couldn't feel any remnants of it left at all. It was like a veil had suddenly been lifted and the hold the room had on her soul had been released… temporarily.

"Did you see her?! Did you *see* her?!" she cried desperately, hyperventilating. "She was right there! I saw her right *there*! Did you see her?"

"Did I see who?" Charlize asked annoyed as she rolled her eyes and began rummaging through the linens to find towels to clean up the water all over the floor. "There's nobody here but you, waking the dead with all that noise."

Aleera swallowed what little spit was left in her parched mouth past a vast lump that had risen in her throat. She pulled herself out of the water, her body shaking like a leaf. Charlize smirked as she tossed her a towel.

"Bad afternoon, huh? Well, don't you fret. Storms out here can do that to a person. Scare the bajeezus out of you if you aren't careful."

She smiled politely and Aleera stared at her with wide eyes.

"Anyway, the cook is preparing fried Catfish and Crawfish Etoufée for dinner. That should make it all better. Nothing like a good meal to get you feeling comfortable again in a spooky old house, right?"

Aleera glared at the maid hating the very air she breathed.

"You're doing this to me, aren't you? You're trying to scare me out of this house! You think you can scare me?"

Charlize rolled her eyes and gave a light chuckle as she began wiping up the floor.

"Now *why* would I want to do a thing like that? Really, *Madame*, you have some imagination on you."

Aleera approached Charlize slowly, her chest rising and falling dramatically. She pointed her finger at the maid.

"I swear to you, bitch, if you ever fuckin' pull another parlor trick on me like that again, I'll rip your fuckin' throat out! Do you fuckin' hear me? You do *not* want to fuck with me like that. You have no idea what I will do to your crazy ass!"

Charlize chuckled again as she stood back up and dusted herself off.

"I'm not too worried about it, *Madame*. Any woman walking around with blue streaks in her hair has to do a lot more than threaten me to get me to take her seriously. But in the future, you may want to stay out of this room. It obviously doesn't belong to you."

The maid smiled politely at Aleera as she folded the wet towel and tucked it under her arm.

"I'll let Mr. LaCroix know that you'll be down to dinner momentarily once you've gotten yourself together. And don't worry, I won't mention that you let something as simple as a bath frighten you. It'll be our little secret."

Charlize said the words sarcastically and headed towards the door of the bathroom, then stopped short. She turned back to look at a shivering, naked Aleera.

"Oh and uh, you know, if I were really the one who frightened you just now, tell me, how would I have simulated those cuts all on your legs, hmm? I'm good, *Madame*, I really am, but even *I'm* not that good. Looks to me you better watch your step around here. Something obviously doesn't want you here and I'm inclined to agree with it. Two hundred years in this house has taught me that you don't go looking for trouble lessen you want to find it."

Aleera frowned, "What? Wait- two hundred years in this house?"

"More or less. But don't you worry, *Madame*, it's really all in good fun. What is it they said in that *Halloween* movie? You know the one with that fella Michael Meyers?"

Charlize pretended to think for a minute then smiled cruelly.

"Oh yeah, that's right. Everybody's entitled to one good scare. But don't worry, I'll have a glass of vodka waiting for you to calm your nerves when you come downstairs."

With that, she turned and headed out of the bathroom, leaving Aleera standing there trembling. Aleera looked all around the beautiful bathroom again. It looked perfectly ordinary- almost to the point where she wasn't even sure if what she'd thought had just happened had actually happened at all. The mirror was clear as crystal. Not the faintest trace of condensation on it. The words were gone... Marielle's face was gone.

"It was a trick to get me out of here," she said aloud to herself. "*She* wants me out."

The deep red cuts stung. Charlize was right. There was no way to fake those cuts. They'd happened. Something about that scenario just didn't sit well. Those weren't the scratches of ordinary nails and they weren't there before she'd gotten into the bathtub. *Something* had attacked her.

She walked out into Marielle's bedroom and looked up at the portrait of the former Lady of the House.

"You won't win, bitch," she spat bitterly. "I'm not going *any*where. I don't give a damn if you jump your anorexic ass out of that portrait and sit next to us at the dinner table. Even then, I'm not going no damn where. I got your man, and I'm gonna keep him!"

She couldn't be sure… maybe it was an illusion or some trick of the light, but it almost looked as if Marielle's portrait had changed from a smug smile to a huge grin. Almost as if to say, *game on*.

CHAPTER IX

Charlize plastered a false, yet convincing smile on her face as she ladled out the night's dinner of Crawfish Etoufée. Savory, spiced, steam swirled into the air offering hungry stomachs something to growl over. The piping hot plate of Fried Catfish was already sitting in the middle of the table, giving off a delicious aroma of its own. Aleera looked at it apprehensively, unsure of whether her stomach, which was tied up in knots and jittery convulsions, would even allow her to eat the delicious smelling food.

She clenched her fists tightly by her side as Charlize came around to pour her an ice cold glass of sweet tea next to her shorter glass of vodka. That sickeningly sweet smile, which in Aleera's mind held traces of smug satisfaction, was still plastered across her lips like a billboard.

"Would *Madame* like anything else," Charlize asked in her politest voice.

Madame Blanchard will have her revenge...

Aleera could see those thoughts dripping from the maid's saccharine smile in green globs. It turned her stomach to stone and made the rage she felt all the more fiery.

"*Mesi*[33], Charlize. You've been very helpful this evening," Nico said elegantly.

Aleera's wild eyes darted over to him. He looked normal enough. He flashed Charlize a charming, dimpled smile- one that wasn't easily resisted. Aleera frowned.

"So, how was your day, *cherie*? I trust that you're enjoying your stay in my home. Is everything to your liking? Is Charlize attending to your needs as I have asked?"

Aleera's frown deepened. *How was her day?* He ought to know how the hell her day had gone. Wasn't he there, smelling like a sewer and ripping through her like some savage ass barbarian? No, wait- that was a dream.

"Well Nicodemus, my day wasn't the best. I feel like I'm starting to lose my mind up in here. I'm seeing things, hearing things... things that aren't there. I'm drinking more than I should..."

---

[33] *Mesi*- Thank you in Creole (Kreyol)

Nico grabbed the hot sauce and poured a generous amount over his catfish and then broke off a piece of honey-glazed cornbread.

"I'm sorry your day was bad, *ma cherie*, but I'm sure that I can be more than accommodating to you this evening. How does a nice massage sound? Maybe relax you a little, hmm?"

He smiled at her with innocence in his eyes and genuine concern. Aleera sighed feeling annoyed.

"I don't think a massage is gonna do it, babe. I need a drink. For real, for real, that would really take the edge off right about now. This little itty bitty glass of vodka ain't gonna do it though. I'ma need the bottle."

"Oh no, *cherie*, that's out of the question. You can't drink like that. Now how would that make me look? Having a woman on my shoulder who needs AA. That certainly isn't the image I'm trying to convey, my love. I think you'll have to make do with the massage."

Aleera took a sip of her vodka and rolled her eyes.

"What the hell happened to you today, Nico? Huh? You came in all bloody and disgusting and you-"

Nico chuckled, entertained, as he proceeded to stuff a bit of catfish into his mouth. He chewed a bit, swallowed and wiped his mouth.

"*Eskize mwen[34]?*"

Aleera scoffed.

"Can you stop talking all that geechee shit to me? I don't know what the hell that means."

Charlize rolled her eyes in disgust.

"Geechees are from South Carolina, *Madame*. This is Louisiana. We're Creole down here," the maid corrected her.

Aleera's eyes blazed at the maid with pure hatred. Nico cleared his throat.

"I apologize, my dear. I'm just very used to speaking it with my wife. It came quite natural for us to speak it to one another."

Aleera sucked her teeth and crossed her arms defiantly.

"I don't give a damn about that! Nobody asked that! *I* don't speak it so don't speak it to me! And I'm still hot with you about today!"

Nico sighed.

"Yes, I can see that you're upset. Obviously some type of hormonal female fit, yes? Is it your time of the month? Again, I offer a massage to help you cope or maybe some *Midol*? That's what they use when it's that time of the month right? *Midol*?"

---

34 *Eskize mwen*- Excuse me (Kreyol)

"What? *Midol*,nigga? Seriously? Nico, what is *wrong* with you? You act like you're not hearing me," Aleera started. She sighed not entirely sure of what she was saying. The dream had been just that, a dream. But then again, it was way too real and Nico *had* been MIA today. Something wasn't right.

"Look, a massage isn't gonna help me. I'm stressed out. The only thing that helps me when I'm stressed is shopping and liquor. So yeah, I'm gonna need some paper so I can hit the shops tonight. *Michael Kors* is having their annual sale, anyway. I need new gear and I need to hit the liquor store cause this puny ass bit of liquor ya'll got up in here ain't doing shit for me."

Nico said nothing. Just kept chewing.

"But for real though, if you really want to make me feel better, you need to get rid of Charlize. She's stressing me the fuck out. She's always making trouble, trying to scare me to death playing practical jokes and shit like that while I'm bathing. I don't trust her crazy ass and she's probably a lezbo anyway, looking at me naked and stuff while I'm in the tub. I know one thing, if she try that shit again, shit is gonna get gully up in here."

"Nonsense," Nico said dismissively as he took a drink of his tea. "I would no more get rid of Charlize than I would get rid of this house. She and her family have worked in this house for years. Two hundred years to be exact. Longer than you or I have even been alive. No... I'm sorry, *ma cherie*, but she stays."

Aleera cut her eyes at Charlize whose face was still plastered with that sugary, fake smile.

"As for shopping," Nico continued, "you're such a beautiful girl, Lee. Beautiful and stacked in all the right places. But if you're going to shop, I think it prudent to have Pierre tag along with you and have him pick out your clothes for you. You see, your style is a little... how shall I say... trashy. Certainly you're aware of my campaign, and if you're going to be by my side, we'll have to polish your image just a tad. And might I add, polishing that image will include slowing down on the drinking. I can't be seen with an alcoholic."

Aleera's breath caught in her throat.

"Wh... what? Change my image?"

"Yes, my love, change your image. It's time to get serious and put aside this trashy little persona you put forth when you were a singer. I know it was sexy back then and sex sells, but let's be honest here. Your career is dead. You haven't had a hit in quite some time. So really, you're just walking around looking like a prostitute for no reason. So you see, we need to banish that horrible image, especially if you someday hope to be my wife."

"Just what the hell is wrong with my image, Nicodemus? You don't seem to have a problem with my image when you're fucking my brains out!"

Nico cringed at her words and shook his head.

"Ugh, I think we might see about getting a few speech lessons for you as well. It just won't do to be seen in public with someone who speaks the way you do when everyone is so used to seeing me with my perfect Marielle. I'm going to be Senator of Louisiana very soon, Aleera. Don't you think that you need to start practicing how to be a lady?"

Aleera's eyes glazed over with the tenderness of her hurt feelings which she tried to mask. Who the hell did he think he was telling her how to dress and how to talk? After all she'd been through that day, he was lucky that she didn't go upside his head with a pistol.

"Practice being a lady," she spat. "How about you practice being a gentleman! You just raped me earlier today and you wanna talk about being a lady? You ain't nothin' but a stone's throw away from ghetto fabulous your damn self! The pot calling the got damn kettle, black!"

Nicodemus chuckled heartily and took a bite of his Etoufée, unfazed.

"Me? Rape you? Don't be stupid. What reason would I ever have to rape you when you give it up so easily that all I have to do is smile at you for a taste? Haha, please!"

That stung. Her face clouded over with pain and embarrassment as misty tears gleamed in her eyes. Nico didn't seem to notice.

"Now listen to me very carefully, my love. At noon tomorrow, Pierre will take you to Bloomingdales to have your wardrobe redone. I expect you to look like a respectable lady when you come home because I certainly can't have you on my arm if you look like a common whore. I'm going to be Senator of Louisiana, after all, and Senators don't hang with whores. Well... at least not whores that look like wanton video vixens. Anyway, following your shopping trip, I'll have Pierre take you to have your hair and nails done. Make sure to pick out a tasteful design for your nails, maybe a French manicure. And as for your hair, long, cascading curls accented with a beautiful, white Magnolia blossom is what I like best. None of that blue hair or bleached blonde shit that I've seen you wearing lately."

Aleera couldn't believe her ears. She stared at him in disgust, her mouth turned up into a tight scowl. Was that really what he thought of her? Nico smiled at her lovingly.

"You'll look beautiful. Just like *her*."

Aleera threw down her spoon and linen napkin.

"Oh hell nah, you got me all fucked up!" she exclaimed ready to go off. She took a gulp of vodka and pointed her finger at Nico. "Let me tell you something about yourself you faking muthaf-"

The lights suddenly flickered as the storm raging outside threatened to leave them in total darkness. Aleera stopped short remembering how the lights had flickered in her dream.

The lightning flashed, crackling and shredding the sky with fierce anger, making Aleera shiver. Charlize returned to the dining room with two plates of French pastries filled with apricot jam and a dusting of powdered sugar on the top as if nothing at all was happening. She made her way over to Nico first and sat the plate in front of him.

"*Mesi*, Charlize," Nico said politely.

Charlize smiled at Nico warmly, then proceeded to make her way down to Aleera. The thunder clapped again, rattling the chandelier like an earthquake had struck. The lights flickered twice more, then extinguished themselves completely.

Aleera gasped at the sudden darkness, feeling that shadowy, dreaded Evil creep up her spine like a spider with prickly legs. It made the skin on her back and neck grow tight and itchy. All that could be heard was the thunder. Everything else was piercingly silent. Then there were those eyes... Those bright, hazel eyes that burned a malicious creamy jade with a speck of gold, seared through the blackness with burning hatred. They were there- bright as day, but then, they weren't. It was a feeling. A deep, horrible feeling of those eyes watching her. And then came the gurgling in the back of the throat... That wretched sound of a person fighting to breathe in dark, murky water...

"Aaaagh! Graaaap!"

Aleera shrieked like she'd been scorched with a red hot poker and came crashing to the floor, tumbling out of her chair. She had to get away from those eyes. *Her* eyes... The lights were suddenly back on.

Nico rushed to her, concerned and confused.

"Are you alright, *cherie*? It's just the storm messing with the electricity. Nothing to be frightened of, I promise. Everything will be alright. Did you hurt yourself?"

He offered her his hand, but it was the decaying hand of a corpse. The skin grew nasty and grey right before her eyes; and red, festering sores with yellow pus began to ooze. Chunks of grey flesh dribbled from the yellowed bone like heated chicken fat. Then it grabbed her, yanking her arm towards it roughly.

Aleera's mouth dropped open as if to let out an iron scream of terror, but no sound escaped. Nico's eyes rolled into the back of his head, disappearing into the black, hollow, holes of a skull; and his mouth twisted into an ugly, toothy grimace.

"You... will... diiiie! Hahahahahahaha!"

It cackled horribly like a demon.

"Oh my God! Oh my *God*! Leave me alone! Get the fuck away from me!" she screamed frantically, clawing to pry the deadlocked fingers off of her arm.

Nico blinked confusedly as he looked at Charlize who had just sat his pastry plate down in front of him. Aleera was still sitting at the table waiting for her dessert. She gasped as she looked back on the floor where she'd just seen herself. There was nothing there at all.

"Aleera? Aleera are you listening to me?" Nico asked sounding irritated.

"Wh- What? I- I..."

"I said I don't mean to insult you but surely you understand what I'm saying about your image. If you ever expect me to marry you, you'll have to conform. Don't you see?"

Aleera rubbed her hands down her face slowly. What was happening to her? Was she losing it?

"Is there something wrong, Aleera?" Nico asked. "You're acting really strange today. You're not even listening to a word I'm saying and you're talking nonsense! You've been bugging me about marrying you for months, and now that I'm telling you what must be done, you're ignoring me!"

"I- I'm sorry. I thought I saw... I- I know I saw something."

"What?" Nico asked. "What are you blabbering about?"

"You know you saw what, *Madame*?" Charlize asked amused.

Aleera glared at her. Maybe it was a trick. Maybe Charlize had put something in her Etoufée to make her see things. Maybe it was a hallucination. Yes, that's what it was. Nothing but a figment of her imagination. After all, she'd been all wound up from that conversation she'd had with Charlize earlier. All that talk of curses and revenge had probably stressed her out so bad that now she was hallucinating. Yeah… hallucinating and dreaming crazy things.

She looked down at her arm where the dead hand had grabbed her. A chunk of the decayed flesh was still stuck to her arm on top of the purple bruises that were now there.

"Oh! God! What the fuck is that? Do you see that?"

She swiped frantically at the chunk of flesh trying to get it off her arm. She was swiping and patting and scratching like her arm was on fire. Nico looked worriedly at Charlize, who shrugged.

"Um… Aleera, what's going on with you? What's the matter? I really think it's time that we take a serious look at your alcoholism. You're starting to take it too far, now. This could really hurt my image at the polls. You don't even make sense anymore."

Aleera looked down at her arm again and there was nothing there. Just the purple bruises and the scratches she was digging into her own arm. She whimpered from frustration and shook her head unsure of what was real and what wasn't.

"I- uh... I- I don't feel well that's all. It's nothing. I just need to..."

She rose from her chair to leave still staring at her arm.

"Wait a minute. Aren't you forgetting something, *cherie*?" Nico asked.

"What? What am I forgetting?"

He chuckled as if it were obvious and gestured with his hand.

"You're forgetting your manners, of course. A lady always *asks* to be excused. She doesn't just leave. Oh, don't worry dear, I'll have Pierre enroll you in a few etiquette classes too. You'll be good as new in no time. Then I'll introduce you to New Orleans Society. They'll love you! That is, of course, if we change that horrible image of yours and get that drinking under control. But don't worry. I promise all will be well. Doesn't that sound excellent?"

Aleera's heart dropped. What the hell was he talking about? She looked at him with an expression of disgust, like he didn't smell good.

"Nico, I really could give a fuck what you're talking about right now. I need to be excused, okay?"

"Would *Madame* like me to summon a doctor," Charlize asked, her face laden with false concern. "I mean since you're so sick that you can't eat your dinner."

"Oh, Charlize! I think that would be an excellent idea," Nico began. "It's so good of you to be worried about your *Madame*. Let's call Doctor-"

"No! I... I don't need a doctor."

"What about a few of my home remedies? I have a few remedies that have been passed down to me over the centuries. Some of them have taken decades to perfect, but they do the trick. Would *Madame* like me to whip her up a special concoction? Something to calm the nerves?"

Nico beamed with pride at Charlize, ecstatic at how caring for Aleera she seemed. Aleera stared at Charlize with daggers in her eyes. The last thing she needed was for Charlize to poison her.

"No thank you," she said through clenched teeth. "I just really need to lie down. It's been a long day and I'm... I'm not sure about everything that has happened. I just need to get some sleep or something. I've been awake too long."

Nico smiled pleasantly and nodded his head.

"Of course, *cherie*. Yes, please get some rest. Charlize, would you see Aleera up to her bedroom so that she-" Nico started.

"No! I don't need her fuckin' help! I can do it on my own! I'm not your precious Marielle that needs a servant to lick my ass for me! I can see my own self up to my own damn room. Gawd! You people think you need servants to do everything for you around here! What is she gonna do? Hold my fuckin' hand while I walk?"

Nico looked at Aleera stunned for a moment. She really *did* need those speech classes. Charlize smiled haughtily to herself knowing that she'd gotten under Aleera's skin.

"Well... fine. Get some rest, Aleera. But you stay out of the Swan Room, you hear? You make sure you don't go in there at all... ever! And that's not a request, Aleera, that's an order!"

Just with Nico's words, the black dread moved its way back into Aleera's chest and turned her bones to stone. Thunder crashed into the darkened clouds of the night, as the lights threatened to blacken the room once more. And there were those eyes... still there, piercing right through her. Still watching her every move... hating her very existence...

She didn't care what Nico said. He could huff, puff, and stick his chest out all the way to hell if he wanted to. None of that was gonna keep her out of that Swan Room. Whatever Evil had attacked her today, it all started in that God forsaken shrine to Marielle and she wasn't gonna take that shit lying down.

CHAPTER X

Aleera reached out to touch the gold handles to the white double doors of Marielle's room, but instantly took her hands away. What the hell would she find in that room? She had already been attacked once in there- at least she thought she was. In all honesty, she still wasn't sure. Common sense should have told her to get the hell out of dodge, but from what? It was very possible that nothing at all had ever happened. Things were just so fuzzy and blurry. She had to be sure- sure of whether she was crazy or if she was being gas lighted. Either way, she was going in that room, do or die.

Taking a deep breath, she opened the door slowly. She told herself that she wasn't afraid, and she sincerely hoped that she meant it because if she didn't, there was no telling what might happen. Slowly, she walked into the room that she suspected was the hub for evil energy in the house.

The Swan Bed still sat on its marble pedestal looking as perfectly regal as it always had. The room was now perfumed sweetly with the scent of creamy lemon, vanilla, and honeysuckle- the signature scent of Magnolias.

Aleera swallowed, feeling fear take over again. *This shit is unnatural…*

She walked about the room again, feeling drawn to it. It was calling to her again, compelling her to stay inside. She remembered the feeling earlier in her dream when she'd tried on the dress and felt afraid, but she was powerless against it then, and even more powerless against it now. She pinched herself just to be sure. Yep, she was definitely awake this time.

She looked up at the portrait, feeling those hazel eyes watching her again. Marielle's face in the painting hadn't changed, but then again, yes it had. That stoic Mona Lisa smile that she wore on her face was now cocked to the side in amusement. There was a mischievous spirit in those hazel eyes- a spirit that was very much alive in a still oil painting. And they stared at her, challenging her without ever saying a word. Aleera swallowed.

"I'm not afraid of you," she whispered, knowing damn well that she was lying. "And I'm *not* leaving. I don't care how much your dead ass bitches and moans. A dead bitch ought to stay dead anyway. Why the hell you worrying about a man and you're somewhere rotting in a coffin?"

The air in the room suddenly grew colder. *Shit!* The Evil was coming. She'd have to hurry or risk another horrible manifestation, but hurry to do what? She wasn't in control anymore. The closet called to her for some reason or another, and she'd just have to see what was in there before it was too late.

Aleera quietly opened the doors to the closet and hurried inside. She wasn't sure what she was going to see, but there was something there. *Something…* she could feel it. It urged her on like a molester lures a child, but a voice in her head told her that she was going too far.

Leave this place or face a fate worse than death!

The voice was a sharp whisper… sharp and icy. The words sliced through the air like a blade and almost hurt to hear. The closet was growing colder and colder by the second. Aleera's heart beat like a thundering race horse's and it made her feel jittery all over.

She'd never faced anything so terrifying in all her life. Not even when she'd been working in the strip club and her boss, Cream, had gotten gunned down by some local drug dealers in front of everyone. It was pretty scary to watch someone get gunned down like cattle, but even *that* didn't seem as bad as this.

She reluctantly reached out to touch the wall, instinct telling her to do so. She felt behind the glittering dresses and gowns, running her hands up and down the wall. *It was there. It had to be there*! Why else did the room call to her like it did? It wanted her to see. It wanted her to know

A latch clicked. Aleera's hands trembled. She didn't know what she'd touched, but a panel in the wall of the closet screeched open, squealing on its hinges. Hot, stale, bitter air rushed at her in a whoosh as if the secret room were exhaling its toxic breath. It made her mouth dry and sour. It had been some time since that door had been opened. Maybe it had been sealed for a reason.

Her body shivered. The cold spots and the hot air from the hidden room sent chills up and down her spine. She took a deep breath and stepped one foot inside the secret room. A thin, threaded film of cobwebs swept across her face like silky fingers.

"Eeeek!" she screeched, fighting off the cobwebs with all her might, swinging her fists in jabs, punches, and uppercuts.

"Oh my God, what am I doing? What the fuck am I doing? This is crazy! This bitch can have Nico! Fuck it! He ain't worth all this."

Aleera exhaled, trying to regain her composure and was ready to run away. But no, she couldn't. She wasn't going to let Marielle get the best of her. She'd never backed down from a stuck-up bitch before, and she'd be damned if she was gonna back down from one now... especially a dead one.

She took a deep breath feeling insane for what she was about to do. Still it had to be done if only for curiosity's sake. She stepped all the way inside the shadowy room one foot at a time and the darkness only seemed to grow blacker. She took a quick swig from her flask hoping that the vodka would calm her down a little. After all, it was just a room. There was nothing to be afraid of in a room.

Her hand brushed up against bookshelves filled with dusty old books. Some of them looked as if they had been there for centuries. They were covered in yellow dust and grey cobwebs; and the smell of moldy, vintage binding was thick in her nostrils. She sneezed.

Hot air blew viciously again from no apparent source, blowing flames onto candles like magic. The secret room instantly lit with an eerie glow that cast shadows along the walls. Aleera's eyes grew wide as the scream that wanted to roar from the depths of her belly tangled itself in her throat, refusing to come out.

Before she could get the nerve to search the room, the wind began to whine and howl, moaning and groaning like it was hurt. Or was that her blood rushing past her ears? She really couldn't be sure. The whining grew louder and louder, sounding more desolate and desperate by the moment. Suddenly, a strong gust of hot air shot through the closet blowing papers, pictures, and books at Aleera from the secret room. She fell to the floor and covered hear head and ears as tears swelled in her eyes.

You will die… You will perish!

She didn't waste any time. She picked herself up from the floor in a hurry and darted out of the closet as fast as she could with her mouth open wide with panic. The papers and books flew through the air angrily like purposeful missiles, aiming right for her head! She frantically slammed the closet doors shut, determined never to go in there again!

"Oh my God, Lord! What the hell? Now I know *that* was real!" she exclaimed. "What the *fuck* is going on in here?"

Her heart beat fast like a race horse's as she slid to the floor feeling defeated. Marielle's overbearing image looked down on her in amusement with the little smile cocked arrogantly to the side. Aleera looked up at it, struggling to catch her breath and shook her head. She wiped the sweat from her brow with one hand as the other palmed the floor to help her up, but there was something underneath it. When she looked down, she saw an old, faded, photograph.

"Oh God, what now? What is this?"

The picture was old, crumpled, and worn; and it was in black and white. Aleera could barely make out what she was looking at. She squinted at it, studying the three figures standing in dark, hooded robes. They seemed to be staring down at some poor, unfortunate soul on the ground, who looked as stiff as a board with wide, horrified eyes. If Aleera didn't know any better, she'd say he was dead.

"What the fuck? The hell is this?"

She turned the picture to its back and found a date. It read in beautiful script:

Bizango, December 27th 1904.

Aleera looked around, wondering where the picture had come from. It probably came from all the papers and books that had mysteriously flown at her from that secret room. *But how the hell had that happened? Books and papers can't fly through the air all by themselves.* She shook her head and looked back at the closet. Yep, the books and paper were still there in a scattered mess. That hallucination, at least, had been real. So at least she could determine that things were really happening now. It wasn't just her imagination anymore.

"Is somebody in here?"

Aleera jumped at the sound of Charlize's voice and quickly hid the picture behind her back. In a split second, Charlize was standing in the doorway of Marielle's room.

"*Madame*, what are you doing in here? *Mesieur* LaCroix asked me to check on you and you weren't in your assigned room. Are you alright?"

"I'm fine!" Aleera said quickly and a little too sharply.

Charlize looked her up and down, then looked around the room suspiciously. Her face grew dark and grave.

"What are you doing in here? I thought it was clear that you were supposed to stay out. Don't tell me that underneath all that *Maybelline* you have a comprehension problem too."

Aleera rolled her eyes. She was itching to smack the taste out of Charlize's mouth just one more time. She bawled up her face and put her hands on her hips.

"I go where the hell I please, okay? I don't need you telling me what I can and can't do. I'm a grown ass woman, and don't need another mama!"

"I warned you to stay out of this room, *Madame*. What, you thought I said it for my health? I don't like you, that's no secret, but if you know what's good for you, you'll stay away from this room. I don't know how many times I have to say it before you get the point. You *have* to stay away from here or you can forget singing in those sleazy clubs you're always at. In fact, you can forget life all together."

Aleera narrowed her eyes. *Was that a threat?*

"Why should I stay away from it? Huh? Why? It's just a room, right? Why should I be afraid of a stuffy, old, dead woman's room?"

The maid's eyes lost any feeling they had in them, and her face seemed old and all too serious even though she was obviously younger than Aleera.

"I think you know it's more than a room by now, *Madame*. You think those cuts and bruises all over your body are little coincidences? Think that tub scene was just a hoax? I think you know better than anybody that this room means you harm. You can feel it in every bone in your body! I *know* you can. My *maman* always told me that only fools rush in where angels fear to tread and you'll be a fool if you don't listen to me. Stay away from this room. If you care about your life and especially your soul at all, you'll stay away. In fact, you may want to think about getting yourself out this house all together if you plan on living past your next birthday. Things aren't what they seem in this house."

Aleera shook her head, refusing to give in to anything Charlize had to say. Even though her gut twisted and wrenched in a way that told her she needed to get the hell out of dodge, she still couldn't back down from the dumb ass maid who just wouldn't mind her own damn business.

"I'm not afraid of you or anybody else. What do I look like being afraid of a room? Ain't shit you can do to get me to leave here. I ain't scared of this place."

Charlize stepped close to Aleera, inches away from her face looking as serious as she ever had.

"You should be."

"Well I ain't."

Charlize chuckled and turned to leave the room. Aleera caught a glimpse of Charlize's reflection in Marielle's floor length mirror near the Swan Bed. What she saw took her breath away. Charlize's reflection was the reflection of an old, decomposing woman wearing an ancient looking maid's uniform from over a century ago. Her skin hung from her bones and her nails were long like claws. Her course grey hair was pulled into a bun, and she was hunched over like she was barely able to walk.

"Oh my God!"

Aleera looked at the real Charlize who looked perfectly normal and as beautiful as ever, then back at her reflection which still showed that of an old, decayed woman.

"Like I said, you should be. Enjoy the remainder of your night. It may be your last."

CHAPTER XI

Nico stood holding a huge, black umbrella to shelter himself from the rain. He didn't want the slightest bit of drizzle to touch the tailor made suit that he always wore in front of the cameras. Even now, he was waiting to give a speech for his campaign and that suit needed to look spectacular. After all, how would he convince the people that he was worthy of being Senator if his suit had raindrops on it? If you can't handle a little rain, certainly you can't handle a whole damn state.

He stood next to his wife's family vault in the St. Louis #1 Cemetery. In his mind, there was no better place to give a speech on how he could help the economy than at his own wife's grave. It was perfect. And he knew the people would appreciate that he took time away from grieving his wife just to speak on the state of affairs in the State of Louisiana.

The air at the grave was thick with the perfumed scent of Magnolias, making his heart feel heavy. He missed her face. Missed the way that her hazel eyes would flash with green fury after realizing that he'd cheated on her yet again... It was that very passion in her eyes that he hoped to invoke during the day's speech. A passion he knew would inspire the people…

He stood with his head bowed in prayer at the Blanchard Family's vault.

"This is ridiculous. You know that right?" Lucien asked. "This whole thing has turned into a circus."

"Shhh! Not while I'm talking to the Big Guy Upstairs."

"You're an idiot. Now suddenly you're religious after all you've done?"

Nico said nothing, just kept his head bowed as he mouthed words silently.

"You're not really praying, Nico. I don't even know why you're going through this charade. Who are you trying to impress," Lucien asked.

Nico groaned.

"Take a hike, will ya? I'm preparing for my speech and I don't need your negativity giving me bad energy! Go stand in the crowd and wait."

Lucien blew a raspberry. He looked out amongst the sea of tombs and saw no one. Not one soul was there to watch Nico give a speech.

"I don't know if you've noticed, but um, we're in a cemetery. A resting place for dead people... and I'm pretty sure that no Senator in history ever gave a speech in a morbid ass cemetery."

Nico ignored his brother and crossed himself.

"Are you seriously expecting people to vote for you? You can bet your ass you're not even on the ballot."

Nico sucked his teeth wanting to knock the hell out of his brother. Why did he always have to diss him like that? He'd been doing it for years... stamping on his dreams. But no matter how angry he was at Lucien, obviously he couldn't hit his brother in front of the cameras. Then he'd really be out of the Senator's seat. He simply smiled and waited to begin. He cleared his throat ceremoniously and smiled at the crowd.

"Dearly beloved," he began. "We are gathered here today-"

"That's for weddings, numb nuts."

Nico felt a hot flush of embarrassment surge through him like a drug.

"Oh uh... I- I mean... uh good people of New Orleans, Louisiana, thank you so much for coming to hear me speak today on the issues that really matter," he gave a charming smile as the cameras flashed, and then raised his finger philosophically.

"I say to you today, my friends, so even though we face the difficulties of today and tomorrow, I still have a dream. It is a dream deeply rooted in the American dream. I have a dream that one day-"

"That's Martin Luther King, asshole," Lucien said sarcastically.

"Shut up! Just shut the hell up!"

Nico felt himself losing control. He looked out at the faces of all the people staring at him in shock and surprise at his outburst. *Calm yourself, Nico before you lose it*, he could hear Dr. Thibideaux say. He cleared his throat nervously and wiped his brow as a few paparazzi snapped pictures.

"I- I'm… please excuse me, ladies and gentlemen. As you can imagine, I'm a little nervous."

"Nico, are you crazy?" Lucien asked gesturing at the crowd of no one. "Open your eyes and look around, fool! There's nobody there."

None of the vaults in the cemetery had anyone beside them mourning loved ones. None of them had any potential voters come to hear the solutions to issues from a future Senator either. The misty rain trickling down to the ground only served to make the various rows of vaults seem more solitary. They were, indeed, all alone.

"Can't you see I'm trying to address the people? Shut up or I'll have security throw your ass out of here," Nico exclaimed through clenched teeth from the corner of his mouth, not wanting everyone to hear him. "I swear! You and *Maman* bully me into making a name for this family, and then when I try to do that, you try to make me think I'm crazy. Make up your damn mind! Either you want me to be Senator or you don't!"

With a huff, Nico turned back to the huge crowd of people, jammed pack between the cemetery vaults, hanging onto his every word. There were so many of them huddled tight beneath umbrellas waiting to hear from their future Senator, that many of them were elbowing and pushing their way through the crowd just to stand near him.

"Pardon the interruption, everyone. I do apologize. As I was saying, four score and seven years ago, our fathers brought forth on this continent a new nation, conceived-"

Lucien shook his head.

"Now this fool is channeling Abraham Lincoln," he muttered. "Can't believe I have to claim this crazy fucker as my brother."

Nico gave him a stank look, "What did you just say?"

"I said you don't have the sense you were born with! You're wasting time! There's nobody listening, Nico! You're quoting Martin Luther King and Abraham Lincoln in the middle of a cemetery! Not to mention, we're standing in the damn rain talking to absolutely no one! That doesn't sound crazy as hell to you?"

Nico plugged his ears with his fingers defiantly, dropping the black umbrella. Lucien wasn't going to make him angry today with all his shenanigans. He simply would refuse to listen and see how his brother liked that!

"La, la, la, la, la! I can't hear you!" he exclaimed childishly in a sing-song voice. "You can't make me! I can't hear you!"

Lucien threw up his hands in defeat.

"That's it. You've lost your mind. There's no hope for you. And to think I stuck by you all these years."

"I can't hear you! I can't hear you! You can't make me! You can't make me!"

Lucien rolled his eyes and sighed, "…idiot."

"Uh, excuse me, did you just say something," a soft voice called out to him. "Are you talking to me?"

Nico turned around quickly to see a woman standing behind him who had obviously been walking by and heard his argument with Lucien. Probably going to a family member's grave to grieve... He saw it as another opportunity to gain a new voter. He cleared his throat and straightened his tie after he took his fingers out of his ears.

The woman was beautiful but wore a look of extreme confusion on her face. Nico suddenly felt stupid. He'd have to remember to scold Lucien about it later. It was *his* fault.

"Oh! I'm sorry," he said feeling the words lost in his mouth. "I- uh... I was just paying my respects to my wife. Uh... she- she uh... died... back... some m- months back."

He'd completely forgotten about the campaign speech that he was supposed to be giving to the cemetery full of nobodies.

The lady smiled warmly and touched his shoulder.

"My sympathies. You sounded really strange a moment ago, but now I understand. I know how hard it can be to lose your spouse. Sometimes it can take you to a really weird place. I should know. I lost my Bernard just last winter. He'd got the cancer, you know."

Nico nodded his head. He could see Lucien out of the corner of his eye, standing with his arms folded, making a face. He obviously didn't approve. Nico ignored him and extended his hand to the pretty lady.

"Nicodemus LaCroix. Pleased to meet you."

"*Anchante*[35], *Mesieur* LaCroix. I'm Adelaide Lafon," the woman replied, shaking Nico's hand.

Her sweet scent swirled in waves around Nico. His eyes lowered in ecstasy intoxicated by the smell. He adored voters who smelled good.

Adelaide looked over Nico's shoulder at the grey, stone vault. It was an old one.

"This is the vault of *La Famille Blanchard*. They're such an old, fascinating family! Your wife, she was one of them?"

Nico looked at the vault and nodded.

"Yes. Yes she was. Marielle Blanchard was her name. She was the last of 'em."

Adelaide's eyes grew wide as she looked Nico up and down.

"*Me zanmi*[36]! I've heard of *Madame* Blanchard and her family! You're a brave man, *Mesieur* La Croix. I heard the Blanchard Family was very powerful at one time. They brought the secrets of Haiti here with them. Terrible secrets."

Nico chuckled at the absurdity.

---

[35] *Anchante*- Pleased to meet you in Creole (Kreyol)
[36] *Me zanmi*- Oh God or Oh my! To express surprise in Creole (Kreyol)

"Hahahaha! Secrets? What secrets," Nico asked. "Marielle, bless her soul, never kept a secret in this world from me."

Adelaide shook her head and smiled.

"I'm sure you're right, *Mesieur*. It's all very silly. They're just old stories. You know in New Orleans, everybody loves a good ghost story."

"Well, now you've piqued my interest. To be quite honest, though my Marielle and I were married for ten years, I admit that I really don't know much about her family. Especially not any old ghost stories... Please, do share."

Adelaide smiled again and rubbed her arm nervously, feeling a sudden chill.

"Well... uh... I just used to hear that the Blanchards knew how to- to do things. Supernatural things... They say that they could make a powder that could turn you into a zombie. Old myths and legends... You know... that stuff isn't real."

Nico tilted his nose in the air to smell Adelaide, not really listening to her words. She *did* smell like Magnolias. Just like Marielle. Or maybe it was that Magnolia tree sitting across the way. Either way, the scent was thick in the air.

"Zombies," he asked, not really interested. "Ha! The reanimated dead? Imagine that. If you knew my

Marielle, you'd know she wasn't into anything that wasn't beautiful… and especially anything that's dead. She was a lady who loved only beautiful things, just as I love beautiful things. And you *are* very beautiful, *Madame* Lafon."

"Uh- uh, thank you, *Mesieur* LaCroix," Adelaide responded feeling uneasy. "That's very kind of you to say."

Nico nodded, smiling creepily.

"You remind me of my wife. She was gorgeous. The true definition of a Southern Belle… just as you are… And the two of you smell similar. Like sweet, blossoming Magnolias."

"Uh- uh- th- thank you, *Mesieur*. I am quite sure that no woman living or deceased possesses the beauty of the Blanchards, though. Their beauty is legendary."

The creepy smile never left Nico's face and Lucien covered his face with his hands. He knew just how it would end. *Madame* Lafon shifted nervously and pushed her hair away from her face.

"I… uh… didn't mean to disrespect your wife's memory with that talk of her family. It's just what us kids were told growing up to scare us and.-. and uh, I had never met anyone who actually knew them personally so… I- I guess I was just a little too curious. Forgive me."

"No need to apologize, *Madame* Lafon. I take no offense. As I said, you're just as beautiful as my Marielle. You look so much like her. She had the same hazel eyes and full pouty mouth. And your skin…"

Adelaide backed away from Nico feeling suddenly uncomfortable, maybe even afraid. It was impossible to pinpoint, but somewhere in their conversation, he had changed.

"Wh- what," she asked in a shaking voice.

Southern trees bear a strange fruit… Blood on the leaves… And blood at the root…

There it was! Her voice! Her beautiful, melodic voice! Yes! She was approaching him through Adelaide. Adelaide was Marielle!

"Oh Mari, is she the one? Is she the one you want me to have?" Nico asked suddenly preoccupied with the voice he was hearing, making absolutely no sense at all.

"*Mesieur* LaCroix, is something wrong?" Adelaide asked sensing danger. "Are you alright?"

Black bodies swinging in the Southern breeze…

Nico stared at Adelaide, drinking in her beauty. And there it was! The Magnolia in her hair… It seemed to suddenly appear out of thin air. It was a sign. She was meant to be his. He was meant to meet her and it was Marielle who had brought her to him.

"Mesieur LaCroix?"

Strange fruit hanging from the Poplar Trees...

A widespread, evil smile eerily crossed Nico's lips. There was a sudden crack, a fleshy rip, and then a spray of fresh, red blood against the grey stone of the Blanchard Family Vault.

CHAPTER XII

Nico staggered into the grandeur house as if he were drunk, covered in blood and feces yet again. His eyes were glassy and moist. He'd been crying like a newborn baby. He really hadn't meant to do it *this* time. Something inside him just urged him to kill her- urged him to see her blood in contrast to that white Magnolia blossom. What was the harm in that? Red against white… How could he have known that it would end the way that it had?

Aleera ran down the stairs at full speed as she grabbed her purse, tucked it securely under her arm, and intended to head out. She took a swig of vodka from her flask and sighed as the liquid soothed her nerves. She hadn't bothered applying makeup or throwing on any designer clothes. Labels certainly weren't going to save her so what good would wearing them do her?

She needed answers and fast. The longer she waited, the more dangerous that house would become. She had had a brief thought of just saying to hell with it and just leaving... Just leave Nico and all that crazy shit behind... Hell, she wasn't one of those bleached blond bimbos in the movie who never knew when to get the hell out of town when the killer was coming for them. Nah, she was smart. Every instinct in her body was telling her to leave Nico's dumb ass there and let him go for self. There was just one problem. Where the hell was she going to go?

Her landlord surely wasn't going to let her back in her penthouse, and she sure didn't have a dime to her name to rent another one. As much as she hated to admit it, she needed Nico, and boy was that damn hard to admit. But the truth was she'd just have to find a way to survive all the craziness that had been happening in that house...

But how? How to survive it? The first thing she would have to do was make sure that she understood what she was up against. As unsure as she was about what was real and what wasn't, she knew for sure that she hadn't imagined some of that shit. And there was no way in hell she was going to stay in there another minute without knowing what the hell was going on. She was going to find out what was happening in that picture she'd found in

Marielle's room. Whatever was in that picture probably had a lot to do with what was wrong with that house.

She'd thrown her weave into a low ponytail and pulled on a pair of form fitting sweatpants. Shit was too damn ill right now to be cute in her tight jeans and heels. She was just about to fly out the double doors of the great hall to go and get help, when she saw Nico standing in front of them looking lost. His face seemed frightened and distant. Then a smell hit her nose that made her gag.

"Nico, what the fuck happened to you? What is that all over you? And for God's sake what the hell is that smell?"

She rushed towards him, concerned about what he'd been through, but stopped short of hugging him. Bum day or no bum day, she wasn't about to get that mess all over her so that she could smell like somebody's toilet. It reminded her of how he'd come home in her dream. It was like déjà vu.

"Nico! Nico, do you hear me talking to you? I said what in the hell happened to you? You're covered in blood! Are you hurt? Talk to me, Negro! What the hell you done gone and done?"

"It wasn't supposed to happen," he said in a distant voice. "It- it wasn't my fault. She just wasn't the one. But I wanted to see... I wanted to see the red. I wanted to see her painted red..."

"What? What are you talking about? See who painted red?"

"Adelaide… Adelaide Lafon. She was beautiful. So beautiful… And she smelled so good… Soft skin…"

"Hold up! You've been out with some stank ass bitch? You muthafucker! I've been going through this bullshit and you've been out there fucking some hoe!"

Charlize could hear Aleera yelling like a mental patient. She sighed and came to see what the commotion was all about, not that she thought it would be anything big. But she took one look at Nico and instantly knew. He'd gone and done it again. She sighed again and put her hand on her hip irritably.

"*Sa'a fou*[37]! Why does this mess keep happening? Two hundred years and I'm still cleaning up this family's messes! I swear you'd think I was babysitting infants," she scolded, rolling her eyes. "I guess I'll run you a bath, sir. Don't worry. I'll take care of it."

She walked off, leaving Aleera and Nico alone as she cursed to herself about always having to clean up somebody's mess century after century.

Aleera frowned. *Century after century?* What the hell was wrong with everyone? It was like living in a damn mental institution. Everybody was batshit crazy. She shook her head and focused on her boyfriend.

---

[37] *Sa'a fou*- This is craziness… in Creole (Kreyol)

"Nico! Do you hear me talking to you? I asked you were you with some bitch cheating on me! And if you were, I'm going to beat that bitch's ass because I know that she knows you're with someone! Why can't you keep your ashy dick in your pants?"

Nico stared straight ahead. His glassy eyes didn't blink or flutter. They were dead eyes. Aleera felt herself growing more and more enraged.

"Answer me, nigga! Were you with some skank ass trick or not?"

Nico didn't respond. Feeling her anger hitting its boiling point, Aleera smacked Nico on the side of the head.

"I said answer me!"

Nico's eyes suddenly came to life. They were blazing with fury and became infuriated holes burning in his head.

"DON'T YOU EVER QUESTION ME AGAIN, YOU BITCH! I'M THE MAN!"

Aleera sucked her teeth in astonishment with her hand on her hips paying no attention to the danger in his voice and the demon behind his eyes.

"You come home covered in blood and smelling like shit and think I'm not gonna ask questions? Ha!

You've got another thing coming, nigga! You got me all the way fucked up! I'm not 'bout to put up with no-"

She flew to the floor, dizzy and dazed before she could say another word. Nico had balled up his fist and two pieced her right in the face. He stared at her with eyes that had no soul.

"I'm the man of this house! You never question a man! You fuckin' cunts know nothing about Southern traditions! You always gotta test me! I'm a man! I get what I want! I do what I want! And gotdamn it, you will OBEY me or I'll light you on fire and burn your stupid ass to a crisp! Fuckin' schoolyard cunt!"

Nico raised his fist to hit Aleera again, but was suddenly forced to his knees by something unseen. He dropped dramatically, writhing in pain. Lightning seemed to strike his head as a flash of bright light flared in his eyes, blinding him. He keeled over just like he was dead and hit the floor with a sudden thud.

He was jerking it fast- so fast that his hand was almost a blur. He had to do it fast because if Maman caught him, she'd beat him unconscious. He stared down at the girl's lifeless body and how her cloudy, dead eyes locked into space seeing nothing at all.

"Hurry, Nico! Maman and Father Mereaux will be here soon. If they find her here, they'll kill you,"
Lucien warned with dread in his eyes.

Nicodemus' eyes rolled into the back of his head as his testicles became tight with anticipation of a pleasurable release.

"They're coming!"

Nico paid no attention. He jerked and he jerked, feeling himself right there at the edge of an intense orgasm when suddenly the wooden door to the little shack burst open! Maman stood there with her bible toting tyrant of a priest standing beside her. The look on her face was mortification- both at the mutilated dead body on the floor and her son masturbating to it. Her brow creased with fury, shame, and sadness. Her eyes burned with hatred as tears flew down her face in furious streams.

"Oh dear God, take me now!" she screamed.

Nico stared at them both with his eyes wide with fear, embarrassment, and ecstasy. Father Mereaux stared with his mouth in a tight line. He squeezed his bible just a bit tighter.

"Proceed, Nicodemus. Let us expel the demon from your loins so that we can begin redemption."

Nico didn't dare move. He stared at Maman who was crying uncontrollably and calling on the Lord. Father Mereaux approached him cautiously and slowly put his hands on Nico's. He guided the boy's hand back to his penis and began to simulate stroking it.

"Release the demons, Nico. It's the only way. Let me guide you."

Maman crossed herself as she watched Father Mereaux touch her son. Nico suddenly began to get that dirty feeling again, and the craving to do The Bad Thing only intensified.

"Maman, please don't make me!" he cried, not wanting Father Mereaux to touch his penis. "Please, I don't like it when he touches me! Please help me Maman!"

Tears streaked down her cheeks as she clasped her hands in prayer.

"It's the only way, Nico. Dear God, he says it's the only way! Release your demons!"

CHAPTER XIII

Nico opened his eyes suddenly with his body cold with sweat. Aleera lay crumpled on the floor next to him, curled in the fetal position holding her face. He could see the bruise he'd just put there with his fist and instantly felt horrible for it. He touched her tenderly. She flinched.

"Oh please don't be afraid of me, Lee. I need you. I'm so sorry baby. I'm so sorry that I hit you. I'll do anything to make it up to you. Please, Lee! You can't leave me! I need you! I- l-love... I love... Please!"

His shoulders shook up and down as tears streamed uncontrollably down his cheeks. He sat Indian style, rocking back and forth and crying like a baby longing for a mother to love him. Marielle had tried to love him but he had always shunned her in life. Now he found himself longing for that love again with no one to give it to him.

Aleera uncurled herself from a ball and tried to scoot away from him. That nigga had just hit her in the face like she was a man. There was no way in hell she was

about to sit there and listen to him pleading about how
sorry he was. She shook her head no, feeling somewhat
afraid of him.

"Oh, Lee! You're so beautiful. Your face is
perfect. Please forgive me. Please promise never to leave
me. Say it! Say the words! Say you'll never leave me."

He reached down to caress her face and kissed her
bruised cheek. She felt a feeling of warmth surge through
her body as his tear drops hit her face with soft splashes.
Maybe he was sorry.

"I didn't mean to hurt you, Lee! Please! Tell me
you'll never leave me! Tell me!"

"I'll never leave you, Nico," she whispered.

Nico frantically pulled himself to his knees and
grabbed Aleera's hands. Mucus oozed down his nose and
onto his top lip as he gazed into her eyes pitifully.

"Aleera, will you marry me? Tell me that you'll
marry me! Tell me that you'll spend the rest of your life
with me and that we'll die together as one! Tell me now
or I'll die!"

Aleera stared at him. *Was he serious*?

"Say yes gotdamn it!"

He sobbed harder. His nose leaked long ropes of
green snot and his mouth turned downwards like a child's

having a tantrum. He sat there stinking and crying, hoping for some type of sympathy. He looked into Aleera's eyes.

"Say it, Lee! Say yes! Say you'll marry me! That's what you've always wanted! I know it is! You always called me over and over asking me to ask you! Now I'm giving it to you. Say it! Say it or I'll dieeee!" he whined.

Aleera rubbed his back, hoping he'd just shut up. She'd never seen him like that. He was usually so dominating and demanding and now just seemed sort of pitiful... not to mention, annoying. Besides, she wasn't about to marry his ass anytime soon after he'd decked her like that. What kind of shit would that be? She may have been a gold digger but she wasn't about to be an abused wife.

Nico, tired of not having an answer, grabbed her face and brought his to hers, kissing her passionately. It was wet and disgusting. Snot, tears, and thick saliva was smushed all over her face as he gave her all he had. Of course the smell of feces that was still steaming off of his clothes didn't help. Aleera felt her stomach heave as a bit of bile came up, burning her throat.

"Oh God, Nico! Please! Stop! What the fuck? This shit is disgusting!"

"Tell me you'll marry me, Lee! Say it! Say it or I'll fuck you up! I don't wanna do it, but I have to! I'll have to fuck you up if you won't marry me!"

"Yes! Yes! I'll marry you, just take a gotdamn bath! You smell like a hog!"

Nico began hyperventilating, and his eyes rolled into the back of his head. His body shook as his mouth foamed white, and he passed out. Just like that. Aleera gasped, wondering if he were dead. It amazed her that a small part of her (and it was pretty small but still there all the same) wished that he really *was* dead. Maybe then all the drama would be done and over with.

"Charlize! Charlize! Hurry! I think he's dead! Damn it, I killed him! Oh God! Can we forge his signature so that I can at least get the money? Did he make a will? No! What am I saying? Call an ambulance!"

She didn't want to hold him anymore. He smelled terrible. She laid him down on the floor and hurried to her feet. Charlize came running, her eyes frantic. She eyed Nico on the marble floor then looked at Aleera.

"I don't know what happened to him. He came in looking crazy and- and bloody. He was having a fit and fell to the floor, and then he sorta passed out. He's not moving and I can't tell if he's breathing," Aleera stammered out of breath. She didn't know how much more drama she could take in one day. "I swear I didn't kill him! He fell out like this!"

Charlize took one look at him and rolled her eyes.

"Oh please. He ain't dead, *Madame*. *Mesieur* falls into those deep sleeps sometimes when he comes home like this. You know, exhausted and agitated about something or another. You can just leave him there. I'll have Pierre help him to his room. He'll be fine in a few hours."

Aleera searched Charlize's face, but she showed no emotion. No concern. Nothing.

"Charlize, please, I know that you don't fuck with me, but what in the hell is going on in this house? You're acting like all this shit is normal and I keep thinking I'm hallucinating! It's real isn't it? All of it?"

"Look, I'll level with you. I told you to leave and I meant it. Not 'cause I don't want you here, but 'cause this place is not the place for you. It doesn't want you here."

"*Who* doesn't want me here? It's a gotdamn house!"

"*She* doesn't. You have no idea what you're up against and trust me, you don't want to know. This is not just a house. This is *her* house! *Her* soul is in this house. *Her* spirit... And everything bad that happens to you here happens because she wants it to. Believe me when I tell you, you have more to lose than just your life. Trust me, I ought to know!"

Aleera's heart was racing. She'd been through enough fucking around with that house and didn't intend to take much more. Maybe it was time to cut her losses and just leave, whether she had somewhere to go or she didn't. Anywhere was better than there.

"Will you help me, Charlize? Please. Can you help me," Aleera pleaded, sounding uncharacteristically desperate. "I'm sorry about everything. I just really need your help."

"Help you do what? All you gotta do is walk out the door and be done with it. You're free, but instead of doing that, you'd rather hang around here hoping to get some money. *Mesieur* ain't gonna give you no money I can tell you that. You're wasting your time there. You're a gold digger and believe me, a gold digger won't prosper in *this* house. Even messing with *Mesieur*, you're asking for trouble. He ain't who you think he is either."

Aleera opened her mouth to protest, but Charlize shook her head no seriously.

"Nothing I can do, *Madame,* no matter how much you beg. My family has lived in this house for over two hundred years. And for two hundred years, we have been loyal to the Blanchards. I don't get involved in what they do. If I did, it would be my ass on the line just like yours and they've already done enough to me. My soul is at enough unrest. Believe me, I don't want any parts of what you got coming to you. All I can do is warn you, but if you're too money hungry to listen, that's on you. If you stay here, you're dead and it's really just that simple."

"I'm scared, Charlize. I didn't treat you right before and I'm sorry for that, but I'm scared now. Please don't abandon me like that when you know what's going on," Aleera begged.

Charlize could see the worry in Aleera's eyes and felt sorry for the poor gold digging whore who didn't have sense enough to get the hell out of dodge when the shit had clearly hit the fan. She sighed.

"*Bón chans*[38], *Madame*. I really do hope that you get out of here with your soul at least, even if your body does end up six feet under. And from the looks of it, that's exactly where it's gonna end up. But I'll tell you, I'd rather end up six feet under than have my soul enslaved. And that's the truth. *Bon chans*."

Aleera sucked her teeth and threw up her hands feeling frustration, anger, and fear all comingle into stewed emptiness that filled her entirely.

"Speak fuckin' English! At least make this shit make sense!"

Charlize looked her in the eye seriously.

"It means good luck. And trust me. You're going to need every bit of it you can get."

Aleera stared Charlize down, wanting to smack the hell out of her, but was afraid.

---

[38] *Bón chans-* Good luck in Creole (Kreyol)

"You're a cruel bitch," Aleera whispered.

"And you're a dead bitch. Guess we can't all be classy. Ah well. Anyway, I guess I'll go and close all the windows. Real bad storm coming. I can smell it. Night like tonight, a storm is bound to come. And don't you worry about *Mesieur* LaCroix. Pierre will get him up soon enough."

With that, Charlize walked off leaving Aleera alone with her new, smelly fiancé who was foaming at the mouth like an epileptic.

CHAPTER XIV

The rain poured in buckets as Aleera tromped through the wet streets of New Orleans. The storm that Charlize predicted seemed to be well on its way.

She had hurried to get herself out of the house. She wanted to make sure that she was gone before Nico woke up. She needed answers and she wasn't going to sit around waiting for the house… or Marielle…whoever to possess him again so that he could get back to whipping her ass. Damn all that. Those days of smacking her around were going to come to an end if she had anything to do with it.

She had gone to New Orleans. She knew if she were going to find any information on how to protect herself against a spirit, New Orleans would be the place to find it. It was the Mecca of the supernatural.

A little Google research had pointed her in the direction of a candle shop on North Broad Street. Apparently it was likely she would find her answers there. There was a strong voodoo or hoodoo following, and that's where the locals bought their supplies. Aleera wasn't sure what hoodoo or voodoo really was, or even if they were the same thing, but whatever it was, if it could save her she'd try it. She would even cut the head off a chicken if it came down to it...

By the time she'd gotten to the candle shop, she was soaked from weave to toe. Just looking at it, she didn't feel an ounce better than she did when she left the mansion. F&F Candle Shop was an old rundown store that looked like it had probably seen its heyday in the 1950's or 60's. It was dusty with faded siding and broken down shutters. It damn sure didn't look like a place to get spiritual healing.

As she pushed open the old screen door, a cowbell jingled, alerting the owner of her presence. She walked in and instantly noticed that the shop smelled like incense, sweet and spicy candles, and all types of oil. Candles were lit and giving off a pleasant glow. There were pictures and statues of black saints posed in prayer throughout the store. Thankfully, it felt a lot different than it looked. The atmosphere was peaceful and full of tranquility.

A woman wearing a long white Muumuu and white head wrap glided across the store smiling. She was a chubby woman, with oily, round, dimpled cheeks, happy blue eyes, and dark, chocolate skin. She wore a smile so big that it looked like her face must hurt, and her teeth were big like Chiclets. She looked like one of those big women that sang in the church choir.

"*Bonjou!*" she exclaimed happily. "Welcome to F&F Candle Shop! We're here to serve all of your spiritual needs. I'm Ole Marguerite DuBois! Yes ma'am I am! How can I help you today, *chére?*"

The woman was bubbly and immediately likable. She reminded Aleera of someone she wished that she had. A grandmother or an elder aunt- someone who cared… Maybe the woman just had a good spirit, one that sparkled like a beacon in her bright blue eyes. The old woman's scent even reminded Aleera of a grandmother. She smelled like molasses cake or gingerbread with just a touch of cinnamon. Maybe she spent most of her day in the kitchen baking delicious pastries for children or whipping up spells inside of cookies.

Aleera wasn't sure how, but she could practically feel the good nature brimming from her chocolate skin. Aleera took a swig of vodka from her flask.

"Drinking, *chére?* That there is a nasty business," Ole Marguerite said looking concerned.

Aleera opened her mouth to speak but her voice cracked and she fell into the woman's arms dramatically. The floodgates opened and the tears flew uncontrollably. She wasn't sure why in the world she would break down like that in front of a stranger, but in an odd way, she felt she'd come to the right place. Damn sure felt better than Blanchard Manor.

"I'm soooo sorry," she wailed like a baby. "I'm not usually like this! I can hold my own but... now... I... I need help! I don't know what's happening! I'm exhausted and she's gonna kill me, I just know it! It's not enough for her to hurt me. She wants me dead! She literally wants me fuckin' dead!"

The woman's face creased with lines of concern and extreme worry as she wrapped her great, big arms around Aleera who seemed tiny in comparison.

"Somebody done wronged you, *chére*? Who done put the root outchea' on you?"

Aleera's body trembled as she laid her head on the woman's shoulder. She breathed the old woman in, savoring the smell that made her feel so comforted.

"I'm scared! I don't know how roots work but I think maybe somebody might have put one on me before they died! It's a dead person doing this to me!"

The woman rubbed Aleera's back comfortingly like she was a child with a scraped knee.

"There, there, child. Don't cry, now."

The woman wiped Aleera's tears away and smiled at her again warmly.

"You tell Ole Marguerite what happened and we'll see if we can't nip it in the bud!"

Aleera sniffed pitifully and took another sip from her flask. She rubbed her lips with the back of her hand, then downed a bit more liquor before putting the cap on her flask.

"I don't know! I feel like there's some kind of possession in my fiance's house. His ex-wife is dead, but I swear she's in that house! I think… I'm not sure! But I think I know she's there! I feel her eyes watching me! I can feel her laughing! And so many crazy things have happened. My fiancé is acting like he's possessed all the time… coming home looking like he killed somebody. And strange things I can't see are attacking me! Cutting my skin to ribbons! My back! Just look at my back! I didn't do that to myself."

Ole Marguerite lifted Aleera's sweatshirt to examine her back and frowned. She didn't see a thing.

"Well I don' know, *chére*. I don' see nothin' back here but skin."

Aleera gasped and felt her back for the scars she knew were there and found them there all scabby like tree bark!

"They're right there, ma'am! Right there! See! Look!"

Aleera tried to point to the scars she was feeling with her hands. Ole Marguerite looked again but shook her head sadly.

"Nah, I can't say I see anything back there, *chére*. Ain't nothin' but a bit of skin."

Aleera felt her back once more, growing angry at the old woman but suddenly the scars were gone. Her back was as smooth as stone. She gasped, feeling alarmed.

"I swear they were there! They were just there! Just now! She attacked me in a bathtub and scratched me up! I'm not making this up! I mean... I-I drink a lot but-but this is real! I didn't imagine this!"

Aleera sobbed more and Ole Marguerite patted her hand.

"Who done tore off and did this to you, *chére*? Playing with your mind this-a way."

"My fiance's dead wife I told you! I don't know how, but somehow she did this to me! I know it was her! She hates me. Or- or maybe it's the maid! I don't know! I keep seeing the maid and one minute she's young and the next minute she's old! I'm so confused! I don't know what's real and what's not anymore!"

"Who is your fiance's dead wife, *chére*? It's a powerful magic that could do something like this. Only somebody really practiced in the dark side of voodoo could do something like this to you- mess with your mind

and such. Voodoo… or maybe *obeah*[39]. Something…
But whoever did this used a black magic. Black… evil…
The dead can't harm the living lest there be a living person
who sent them. And only somebody evil would do that."

"Her name is M- Marielle B- Blanchard," Aleera
sobbed, sniffing snot back into her nose. "That's who did
it! I don't know what kinda magic she does, but she did it!
But she's dead! Dead and buried! That bitch been dead
and buried for over a month!"

All of the blood drained from Ole Marguerite's
face instantly, turning it from a rich, roasted coffee bean
brown to an ashy grey. She let go of Aleera and moved
her wide body away from her. Her chubby cheeks didn't
look quite so happy anymore.

"Blanchard, you say? *La Famille Blanchard*?"

Aleera nodded not understanding the big deal.

"Oh Lord, child. You gotta gon' get yourself away
from that house. Ain't no love in *that* house. I know that
family, child. The Blanchards… Powerful. And right
scary too. Folks say they knew magic like no others.
They have the power to take your free will away from you.
The power to take your soul…"

It was everything that Aleera didn't want to hear.
For the first time, she couldn't help but wonder if maybe
she'd made a mistake pursuing Nico romantically the way

---

[39] *Obeah*- Jamaican version of voodoo

she had. She certainly *had* known he was married. But fuck! He was so damn sexy. That edible brown skin, and those deep dimples in each of his cheeks… that perfect, pearly white smile that could get her panties moist every time. How could anyone, including his wife, fault her for going after him? Now she was expected to die for it? Oh hell nah! Even with all his sexiness, Nico wasn't worth all that trouble.

"What do I do," she asked hopelessly. "How do I get out of this? I just want out."

Ole Marguerite shook her head.

"Nothing you can do, child, but get yourself away from there and never go back. You go back and they sho' nuff gon' be toting your casket down there to the cemetery in a week. I can tell you that."

Aleera shook her head. "But I can't leave. I have nothing. I have nowhere to go. No money, no home, no nothing. What am I gonna do? Where am I gonna go? What choice do I have but to go back? I just want out of this mess!"

Ole Marguerite shook her head with pity.

"You can't go back there, child. It ain't safe. It'll never be safe again. You don't know what the Blanchards are… what they can do to you. They're nothing like you've ever seen and you have no idea what *hasn't* gotten to you yet. That maid you mention probably the same maid they done had all along. Young gal that they done stole her soul and locked it up in that house. I heard the stories. She gon' be in that house til ain't no house no more. They got that kinda power child, you hear what I say?"

"What? What? I don't even understand what-"

"They're working you, child. You got to listen to me. I can see it in your eyes. And I tell you, it's only gonna get worse. Possessing that fiancé of yours ain't nothin' compared to what gon' happen in the end."

"Well what are they? The Blanchards? Who are they? Who is Marielle Blanchard, really? And Charlize- the maid- what is she?"

Ole Marguerite breathed in deeply and shook her head remembering. That was a question that no one should answer if they knew what was good for them. The Blanchards were a people that she didn't *ever* want to mention again. Truth be told, she wasn't sure if it was even safe to tell the girl what she knew. The last thing she wanted was a battle of the souls with those bloodthirsty people. She swallowed.

"The Blanchards are an old family, *chére.* Much older than most, I can tell you that. Made their money in sugar cane over in Haiti, and after a while, I reckon they got tired of being there and come here. But they a heap more than just a family of sugar cane farmers, that's for sure."

Aleera held onto Ole Marguerite's every word, waiting to hear what type of monster she'd stumbled upon. It was just a matter of time before she was told. Because make no mistake, Aleera could feel deep down in her bones that Marielle was some type of monster.

"Some say that they could put a root on you so terrible that your children's children would feel it for a thousand years. Many people feared them, child. Right many. And in Haiti, they used that fear to control others beneath them… poor folk and all. They say they were a part of a secret society that could rip your soul clean 'way from you… a society nobody dares mention out loud. They used to call 'em *San Pwel*."

"*San* what?

"It means 'without skin.' That's just one name for 'em though. There are many others. Sometimes they go by *Bizango* too. Scary names that people feared…"

Aleera felt a pang of dread in her chest that took her breath away. Just hearing the name spoken aloud sent chills down her spine. She reached in her purse and pulled out the picture she found.

"*Bizango?* Like this?"

Aleera handed the picture to Ole Marguerite. The heavy set woman with the round chubby cheeks gasped in shock. Her hand trembled as she stared at the picture of the hooded figures and the man lying on the ground. Her breathing became erratic and a bit of sweat beaded on her brow. It was a long while before she spoke again. She was becoming more and more unsure about whether she should be discussing this with the girl. You could never be sure just who was listening.

"Whatchu doin' with this picture, child? Lord knows you gon' bring a force down on your head totin' somethin' like this around! It ain't safe!"

"Well what is it? I didn't mean to find it! It found *me!*"

Ole Marguerite shushed Aleera and looked around to see if anyone were watching.

"This picture," she began slowly, as she wiped her lips nervously with trembling hands, "is of a ceremony. They're *Bizango* all right."

Aleera stared at her, noticing the change in Ole Marguerite. The muscles in her face twitched as she talked and her previously bright, blue eyes now seemed to grow darker like a light had been snuffed out within them.

"What kinda ceremony, Miss Marguerite? And what does a ceremony like that have to do with what's happening to me?"

Ole Marguerite clasped her hands in prayer and shook them. Her chest rose and fell.

"Oh *chére*! You done stumbled on something terrible! This ceremony ain't meant to be seen by nobody! This ceremony…" her voice trailed off.

"The ceremony what?" Aleera demanded, losing her patience. "I need to know! What am I up against?"

"It's a ceremony of zombification."

"Zombifiwhat!"

"You heard me right, child. Zombification… the act of making zombies…"

Aleera threw her hands up and rolled her eyes.

"That's impossible. Like… nah, man. You can't be serious. The Blanchards can't possibly… This shit is unreal."

Ole Marguerite waved her hands in the air.

"Shh, child! Somebody'll hear you! We don't speak that family's name. Now listen, you got to believe me. I wouldn't make this up. Zombification is serious. Deadly serious. It's the worst thing they can do to you and trust me, they can do a lot! That maid can tell you!"

Aleera sucked her teeth. She didn't know what she expected to hear, but it damn sure wasn't zombies.

"Nobody in their right mind fittin' to believe some shit like that."

Ole Marguerite looked sad.

"Don't matter if you believe it or not, *chére*. It's real. And that's what's happening in this picture- a ceremony for zombification. And if you know like I know, you'll get yourself out of that house 'fore this becomes you," she said pointing at the man lying on the ground. "'Fore your soul becomes some slave to black magic. It's a punishment- a terrible punishment. And when you cross 'em, they make you a zombie. Take your soul and make it do the bidding of a *bokor*. *Bizango*… they got their own justice. They got their own ways of handling things. Ain't no stopping 'em. They been 'round for centuries doing this mess."

Aleera snorted, laughing. Okay so yeah, Nico was possessed and yes the house seemed to be haunted and she was hallucinating like she was on acid. But zombies? Now she'd heard it all! Zombies were those rotten corpses walking around trying to eat your brain with decaying flesh hanging out of their mouths in movies. That shit didn't exist in real life. Hell, she liked watching *The Walking Dead* just as much as the next person, but trying to say they existed in real life was taking it a bit far.

"This is fuckin' nuts. You can't expect me to buy this! My life is in real danger and you're asking me to believe in fuckin' zombies! Get real, old woman!"

"I ain't asking you to do nothing, child. You came to *me* for help. I'm telling you what this is. You can believe it or not, that's up to you, but all that I've said is true. The Blanchard Family has been involved in this stuff since the slave revolt over in Haiti back in the early 1800's. This is old magic. Centuries old. Old and extremely dangerous. And if what you tell me is true 'bout the things that done happened in that house, I tell you, you done angered them Blanchards. You better hope *all* they do is kill you."

Aleera snatched the picture from Ole Marguerite and stared at it. She couldn't see the faces of the hooded figures, but the man laying on the ground whose eyes stared straight up at the sky, looked dead. Dead or not, his eyes held an indescribable fear in them that looked like even in death, he knew that a savage punishment waited for him. There was no peace in his death.

"But how? How is this possible? How can any of this be real?"

Ole Marguerite wrung her hands nervously. She crossed herself asking Jesus for protection. Telling the girl any of that could be endangering her *own* soul. She took a deep breath and sighed. She no longer looked as cheerful as she had. Now she looked like someone had died... or was about to.

"Sit down, *chére.* I'm gon' tell you a true story of how it all works. I heard this story told to me many a time by my *granmére.* This is how we learned as children never to cross *Bizango.*"

CHAPTER XV

Claude could hear his wife wailing and crying pitifully for him She shrieked and whined like a dying cat at the sight of his beaten down, rickety, wooden coffin being lowered down into the damp ground. His hands were folded neatly across his stomach as he laid there in his second-hand black suit, sweating. Though his eyes had been glued shut with tree gum from a Eucalyptus, it didn't stop sticky tears from streaming down his cheeks as he lay there in still darkness. He was dead. They had declared him dead.

The air in the coffin was so hot and stale that blood trickled from Claude' nose and down his face. Blood, sweat, and sticky tears… He was a mess- a dead mess. His second-hand black suit clung to his body with wet spots underneath his arms and crotch. It was really hot and humid in there.

He could feel the splintered wood scrape the top of his head, legs and hands, making him itch all over. The damn coffin was too small for him. The fit was so snug and tight that even if he could move, the task would have been impossible. It was agony! Not to mention he was claustrophobic. His entire body was on fire with the fear of the closed in walls, but there was nothing he could do. He just had to lie there.

None of his family members seemed to notice that despite the hot, humid heat that should have had his corpse stinking like rotten meat, he smelled just fine- or at least no funkier than everybody else. But no one would have bothered to pay attention to that now would they? They said he was dead so dead is what he was going to be. No one was going to argue it. His wife was too distraught grieving for the husband she thought she'd lost. His brothers were too giddy to take possession of his land and animals so that they could fatten their own pockets and steal his fortune. And his mother, of course, was way too afraid of Bizango to ask any questions. If they said it, then that's what it was. Case closed.

"Claude! Claude! Oh Claude!" his wife cried over and over again, throwing herself at any relative who would catch her.

It broke his heart to hear her crying like that. It broke his heart even more than knowing that his existence had been extinguished. But there was nothing he could do to ease her pain; she'd just have to cry. He would never see her or his children again. Bizango had seen to that. Come that night, his soul would belong to them and his body would be nothing more than a shell... and nothing would be left of the man that he once was.

He struggled to scream, but the sound was muted in his throat by their evil magic. He couldn't move his mouth, nor could he open his eyes. He was trapped in a wooden box that was splintered, too small, and digging into his skin while his eyes, glued shut, kept him in total darkness. His body temperature was rising- maybe from the sheer hell of being locked in a box. Whatever the case, it was certainly making his skin feel clammier and bristly like a thousand fire-ants with their prickly legs were creeping and crawling all over him. It was unbearable! It was torture to be so close to those you love but unable to talk, move, or at least let them know that you weren't completely dead- not completely.

Then came the soft repeated thump of dirt being tossed, carelessly atop his coffin. And with each soft thump-thlump, a bit of dirt seeped through the cracks of the rickety coffin right onto his face. He was reminded yet again, that he was deader than a doornail.

Eventually, the cries of his wife grew dimmer and dimmer until finally, they ceased altogether. They faded away in the blistering heat to nothingness. Now he couldn't even hear the buzzing of mosquitos. No, now there was nothing but blackness and silence for who knows how long. Seconds turned to minutes, minutes into hours, and hours into an eternity.

The air in the coffin grew hotter and the walls seemed to be closing in even more than they already had. It was getting harder and harder to breathe; and his lungs were growing tight and painful. He was beginning to feel dizzy, and his fingers were going numb. Sweat dripped down his forehead and onto the tops of his eyes as he lay there listening to nothing and seeing no one.

Meanwhile they were coming. He could feel them coming. They marched through the dark cemetery like a winding snake carrying large staffs topped with polished, white skulls. Some carried torches to light the way between the graves. All of them wore red and black robes with hoods that obscured their face from view. They were red shadows who paraded into the cemetery to claim their victims.

There was a low hum from their creepy, evil chanting. To the untrained ear, it sounded like humming to the melody of baby's lullabies. But it was anything but a lullaby. The chanting was meant to put fear in the soul, and Claude could feel the chanting in his skin.

Then there was the drumming that grew louder and louder with each passing second. It was a low and steady beat that could stop the heart of a man if it wanted. A few of the hooded figures shook tortoise shell rattles to the beat and hummed loudest of all. One hooded figure carried a coiled, 6 ft long, Royal Python wrapped around his arm. It slithered around and around, licking out its forked tongue like the evil serpent that it was.

Movement slowly began to return to some of Claude's muscles, though his fingers seemed to still feel numb. The lack of oxygen in the coffin was beginning to take affect though, as his fingertips and lips were turning blue. He shook his head from side to side sluggishly, scraping his face against the walls of the coffin. It was impossible to escape before they got to him, but now that he could move, he had to try.

He could feel the beating of the drums in his heart. They were calling to him. Calling to him- commanding him to wake up. Commanding him to wake from the black sleep of death to come to them... Escape was a fantasy in his mind.

He strained to scream, but still couldn't make a sound. His vocal chords remained numb. He could feel them vibrating, but the sound was lost deep within his throat.

Then came that horrible scraping sound! It came faster and faster! Coming closer and closer- closing in on him with that horrible noise that only the most horrific demons in hell could make! Finally there was a hard, metallic scrape against the wood! Shovels scratching the dirt off his coffin like persistent dogs digging for a bone... They'd done it. They'd dug him up!

The hooded figures pried open the wooden box with crowbars, splintering the wood to bits. Claude could feel the sharp splinters digging into his face.

The snake hissed at the sight of the seemingly dead body lying there sweating in the coffin. Just the sound of it made Claude want to piss his pants.

"Claude Jean-Paul Montegut, awake and rise!" a guttural, authoritative voice demanded with harsh cruelty.

Claude' eyes forced themselves open against the stickiness of the glue instantly. He had no control over it. His skin immediately tore, leaving bleeding, painful gashes. His eyes were yellow and glassy as he stared at the hooded figures, frightened. All of his childhood nightmares were coming true.

He felt his limbs work against his will, forcing him to sit up and rise from his grave. The drums rang throughout his body, making it move all on its own. He struggled to scream out but still couldn't make a sound. The powder they'd blown into his face that had "killed" him rendered him unable to control his body.

"Open your mouth!" the cruel voiced, hooded figure hissed evilly.

Slowly, Claude's jaws pried themselves apart, exposing his mouth to the sky. The drums beat faster and faster and the melodic chanting grew louder and more excited. The rattles shook with fierce rhythm as a hooded figure holding a torch took a drink of clairin[40] from a bottle, and spewed the liquor all over Claude' face in a ceremonial spray. Then he spewed the clairin again into the flames of his torch, causing the fire to dance wildly into a fiery blaze.

A few of the hooded figures began swaying to the beat of the drum, seemingly uncontrollably. One of them began to screech rhythmically, as the snake itself seemed to go into a trance. A hooded figure removed a small vial from his inner robes and handed it to the leader. Claude's eyes grew wider and more frightened as he looked all around for someone to help him. There was no one. Everyone's face was shrouded in the shadows of the red hoods.

Fat tears swelled in his eyes. He tried to mouth the words "please" but his mouth remained pried open by a force stronger than his will. He couldn't utter a sound. He was completely helpless.

The leader with the vial approached him slowly.

"Claude Jean-Paul Montegut, you are charged with the crime of opposing the Bizango and have been found guilty. Your punishment is eternal slavery. And your soul will perish in a state of constant suffering!"

The hooded figure dumped the contents of the vial into Claude's mouth then pushed him to the ground.

---

[40] *Clairin-* an alcoholic beverage made in Haiti out of sugarcane, very similar to rum

Claude instantly began to shake and twitch violently as he felt a burning pain shoot through his chest like searing, hot bullets. His mouth gaped open and closed like a dying fish from the unbearable pain, but he was still unable to make a sound. Yellow foam bubbled from his mouth in thick globs as he felt his soul and will-power rip itself from his body like a monster tearing off his limbs. He was bleeding- spiritually... bleeding to death. He could feel the void inside him filling with nothingness as his soul slipped from his body like misty vapor.

Within seconds, it was gone. His skin instantly greyed like that of a corpse. The skin beneath his eyes became dark with deep circles. His eyes, themselves, stared at the sky blankly- lifelessly, looking like glassy, black stone sunken in his head as he lay on the ground. His heart still beat, but he was no longer Claude Montegut. He was no longer anyone- no longer a person. He was a zombie- a slave... and now he belonged to Bizango. Anytime his name would be whispered amongst the lips of children from then on, it would be with fear and pity. Such was the fate of those damned and sentenced by the Secret Societies in Haiti.

CHAPTER XVI

Aleera stared at Ole Marguerite like she was sitting next to a psychopath. You could have knocked her over with a feather.

"Wh- why? Why'd they do that to him? Why didn't anyone stop them?"

"I don't know. Those things are secret. The ways and reasons of the *Bizango* are secret, *chére*. Don't you see? This is how they stay so powerful. They do things like that and nobody sees 'em do it, and nobody knows why. You learn not to ask questions. Questions are a dangerous business. It's just best to stay far away from it and stay far away from them."

Aleera swallowed the little bit of spit past the vast lump that had risen in her throat. Ole Marguerite shook her head remembering as she wrung her hands nervously.

"I had a relative who was turned into one, once. Turned into a zombie... He was a member of one of the sects of *Bizango* or *San Pwel* some call 'em. There are so many sects down there in Haiti, you never know who's who when you're looking at somebody. But all of them *Bizango* follow the same rules. And their number one rule is silence. You don't tell nobody what happens. You don't tell nobody what you see or what you hear, and you don't tell nobody what you do. And everybody who is anybody knows that you never, ever, ever speak ill of them. No matter what happens or what they do. If you speak ill of 'em, they take your soul. Your *ti bon ange*. Just like that. And trust me when I tell ya, ain't nobody stupid enough to save ya."

"I- I don't understand. I- I found a room in the house and there was all these books and papers in there. They all sort of flew at me! Like something out of a horror movie! And then the door slammed shut! That's where this picture came from. Were the Blanchards making zombies in that room? Is that what that room was?"

"Nah, chére. You can't make no zombie in a room. It's so much bigger than that. The power is so much bigger and greater than anything you can imagine. I don't know what that room is, but you best keep out of it, hear? Probably some kind of alter room. I reckon they'd be making sacrifices in there. Probably something like a room for witchcraft, cept' it ain't witchcraft. That's what you got to see. This here is magic mixed in with religion.

It's complicated. This here ain't your world, *chére*, and you best get away from it as fast as you can before it devours you."

"I can't! I have to know what's going on here. I don't know why, but I just have to know."

"Whatchu mean, *chére*? I done told you what I know. What more is there?"

"I need to know how that guy in the story ended up buried alive like that when everyone thought he was dead?" Aleera asked desperately. "How? You have to tell me."

Ole Marguerite sighed and wrung her hands. She looked nervously at the door, then back at Aleera.

"Well, you make yourself a zombie with a potent powder- *coup de poudre* [41]some folk call it. The Blanchards from way back were masters at making it. Whereas *hounguns* and *mambos* are the priest and priestesses of voodoo and they do white magic- magic to help folks, the Blanchards were *bokors. Bokors* use dark magic to hurt people or to control them. That's what the zombie powder is. They make it out of lord knows what, and then blow it in your face or rub it in your wounds... maybe even feed it to you. Within hours, you'd die and they'd bury you."

---

[41] *Coup de poudre*- name of the zombie powder

"But you'd wake up eventually, right? Then they'd know you were alive!" Aleera insisted.

"Nah, ain't no waking up. You'd look dead, you see. And in Haiti, gotta get the dead in the ground before the body starts to stink. It's hot down there and the body can't stay out too long. Got to bury you right away. Ain't no sense in waiting. Not like you gon' get no deader than you already are. That's the logic anyhow. Folk down there can't afford no embalming. That's stuff you do for the rich. Right many of the folk down there are poor, so got to get the dead buried as fast as you can before the whole town smells like rotten meat.

"Anyway, when they are ready to take your soul from your dead body, they go and dig you up. Then they call your name. They call your name with that drum. It pierces your body and goes straight to your *ti bon ange*. Your soul will answer, you see. And they'll feed you the zombie's cucumber. You ain't got no choice but to eat it. That drum commands you to do it. That's the final blow! After that, the process is complete. Your *ti bon ange*, is no longer your own. It belongs to the *bokor* who made you. So long as the *bokor* keeps your soul, you'll be a zombie. Ain't no way out."

Aleera felt like she would pass out any moment. What the hell was she gonna do? How the hell do you even fight something like that?

"But... but Marielle is dead, Ole Marguerite! She's dead! How can she be doing this to me if she's dead and stinking in the crypt? This can't be real."

Ole Marguerite shook her head.

"I don't know, child. But I tell you, if I was you, I wouldn't stick around to find out. They already done got into your head. The soul is a part of your mind. Once they in your mind, it's over. They can give you nightmares so demonic that you'll want to slit your own throat with a piece of glass. You'll want to choke on your own tongue. I've seen it. You'll dream of Death and the Grave. And it will be that way every night! Every hour of every day- every minute of every hour- it'll all be images of Death in your mind. Being a zombie is 'bout as bad as it gets, but make no mistake, that ain't all they can do to you. They can torment you forever."

Aleera looked horrified. Where was the hope? And what about Nico? How was she going to save him?

"What am I gonna do," she asked in a small, frightened voice. "I don't have anywhere else to go."

"Child, aint you getting the point yet? Stay the hell away from that place! What more can I tell ya? What more you need to know? They mean you harm! They mean to kill you physically and spiritually! Ain't nothin' else to say! Why ain't you listening?"

"Please," Aleera pleaded. "Please, I'm begging you. I know you can help me. I know there's something you can do! I'm gonna die without your help! Do you want that on your head?"

"I don't want to get involved, child. Don't you see they'll kill me too? I told you to leave and stay away. I done my part. If you stay in there after I done told you, well then it's your funeral. Ain't nothing else I can do."

Aleera sighed thinking of all the money she'd be leaving behind- all the beautiful clothes. Surely it wasn't worth her life or her soul, but if she could just go back to the house one more time and get the stuff out of there, she'd be home free. All she needed was something to buy her a little time. She gulped, feeling terrified but determined to get her due.

"I just need to get a few things out the house. That's all. I just need you to help me. I need protection for like an hour. In an hour, I can get myself out of there for good. I just need that little bit of time. Please," she pleaded.

Ole Marguerite shook her head.

"You playing with fire, child. I don't like this one bit. Ain't no guarantees. Not even for an hour."

She sighed, her huge breasts rising and falling.

"But if you got to go back, there might be one thing I know that you can do, and it ain't gonna keep you but so safe. Might buy you at most, one hour."

"Please! What is it please? I just need one hour! One hour and then I'm gone forever."

"Yeah, you might be gone forever, child. You said a mouthful there, I'll tell you. Anyway, what you can do is put down some graveyard dust or a little brick dust in your doorway to keep folk away from you who mean to do you harm. That's only gonna stop the living, though. Won't stop nobody crossed over into the spirit world. And if what you tell me is true, them Blanchards got their eye on you from beyond. I got me a little brick dust I can give you, but that's all I can do. Best bet is to get on up out of here and leave that house alone."

Ole Marguerite moved her wide body through the aisles of the store past all the candles and headed behind the counter where she kept her register. Aleera followed her like a lost puppy. What else could she do? It didn't seem to her like crushed up brick would do anything but make a mess on the floor, but she had run out of options and she needed to get back into that house to get Marielle's clothes. Even if she had to get the money, she wasn't going to leave those clothes and purses in there to go to waste, no way.

Ole Marguerite pulled out a paper bag filled with something and placed it in Aleera's hands.

"Take this and put it down in your doorways. Nobody who means you harm can cross it. Even if they don't know they mean you harm, they won't be able to cross it. Don't ever find yourself in a room without this brick dust on the threshold. If you do, it might be the last thing you ever do."

Aleera looked at the old woman desperately. Her eyes were pleading with her.

"Is this all? Can't you say a spell for me or give me something to protect myself? Some kinda weapon?"

"No! I can't do nothing else! You just gonna have to make do."

Aleera fell to her knees crying hysterically. Tears and snot ran together down her face and slimy saliva collected in the corners of her mouth. She grabbed the front of Ole Marguerite's white Muumuu and held on tight.

"Please!" she screamed through sobs and heaves. "Please! They're gonna kill me! They're gonna take my soul! You have to help me! You're all I've got. They're gonna fuckin' kill me!"

"Shhhh! You have to be quiet!" Ole Marguerite commanded as she looked around her store frightened. "Somebody'll hear you and then we'll both be done for!"

The last thing she needed was for anyone to hear the girl. She felt a sudden urge to break down crying herself. What kind of healer would she be if she didn't help the girl in some kind of way? But then again, at what cost was she going to help her? At the expense of her own life and soul?

Ole Marguerite bit down on her huge, pink lower lip. This was a dangerous game. She didn't know what the girl had done to upset the Blanchards, and really, it didn't matter. No person deserved what the girl was going to get in the end when they finished with her. She sighed, worriedly, and embraced Aleera's head to console her.

"Hush now, child. You hush them tears."

Reluctant but determined to overcome her own lifelong fear of Bizango, Ole Marguerite reached up under her counter again and pulled out a wooden box. She'd used it often enough for her customers, but never for this type of protection. She wasn't even sure that it would work, but she had to try *something*. The girl was in serious danger.

Ole Marguerite took out a few items- herbs and such. She began mixing and grinding the ingredients together using a stone pestle and mortar. She then tied the mixture in a small leather-like bag.

"What's that," Aleera asked through snots and sniffles. Her tear stained face was swollen and red. Her eyes had become puffy and she looked nothing like the sultry R&B singer she claimed to be. She looked more like a stressed Cancer patient being read her last rites.

"This is a bit of John the Conqueror root mixed with graveyard dust and a little Deadly Nightshade all ground into the skin of a Royal Python. I grind it to a powder and put it all in the skin of Chamois and tied it with a bit of Devil's Shoestring. It's *gris-gris*[42], *chére*. I'm no mambo and so my magic ain't that strong, but this might offer you a little protection if you believe in it. You keep this close to your skin at all times. If you don't, all is lost. Now I know it ain't much, but this is really all I can do. I ain't got no more advice and no more information for you. And once you leave here, you can never come back. Do you hear me?"

Aleera nodded sadly, and Ole Marguerite tied the *gris-gris* around the girl's neck. The soft leather pouch touched her skin and made it tingle.

"You be careful 'bout who you trust, child. *Se bon ki ra*[43]. Good is rare. Remember that. If you're smart, you'll leave that fiancé of yours behind and get out of town, and you ain't got much time. But you make sure you take the brick dust and *gris-gris* with you. You still gon' need its protection even if you ain't in town. Evil powers stretch far and wide. Now you get on up out of here and may the spirits be with you, child. I'll be praying for you."

---

[42] *Gris-gris*- pouch filled with herbs for protection, luck, love, or powe

[43] *Se bon ki ra*- Good is rare (Haitian proverb)

CHAPTER XVII

Nico stood staring at himself in the mirror feeling completely rejuvenated since he'd finally awakened and had a shower. No more blood. No more shit. His longing for Marielle, however, was becoming stifling and overwhelming. His heart and soul yearned for her and it was almost unbearable knowing that he was the cause of her death.

He could see Lucien's reflection in the mirror, looking at him- judging him. He sighed. He was getting tired of his brother. All Lucien did was tell him how much of a fuck up he was… as usual.

"What now?" he asked impatiently.

"Don't you think it's time that you took responsibility for the things you've done?" Lucien asked seriously.

Nico rolled his eyes. It was always the same ole song and dance with his brother. *Do the right thing, Nico. Take responsibility, Nico.* He was starting to feel like he'd be better off without his brother always around pestering him.

"What do you want from me, Lucien? I'm doing my duty for this family to restore some kind of glory to it. I'm going to be Senator for God's sake. But every time I turn around, here you come busting my balls. What else could you possibly want from me?"

"I have forgiven you for the things you did to those girls, Nico. And I've even forgiven you for what you did to me, but I can not forgive you for what you did to *Maman.* That's something you need to come to terms with. You're still avoiding it like it never happened."

Nico felt his left eye twitch and his body temperature heated up. He clenched his fists and gritted his teeth feeling anger pulse through his veins. He was tired of hearing about *Maman!* She was an abusive bitch who allowed her parish priest to molest him. For his brother to even mention her to him was like committing murder a thousand times. He glared at Lucien in the mirror with fire in his eyes.

"You selfish fuck! Don't speak to me of that *bouzin*! She deserved to die! She deserved what I gave her!"

"You're a disgrace, Nico! She was your mother! The person who gave birth to you! She gave you life!"

"She was a monster! She took my life! She took my innocence! She didn't love me!"

"Who, in their right mind, could love somebody like you, Nicodemus? Marielle was crazy as hell for trying."

Nico growled like a beast and lunged at the mirror, shattering it to a thousand pieces. Lucien laughed maniacally taunting his brother.

"You imbecile! You're even more pathetic than *Maman* said you were."

Nico lunged again, this time at Lucien himself, and found himself crashing into the side of his bed and to the floor. His face was bleeding from cuts and now his side was bruised. Lucien laughed louder.

"I'm a figment of your imagination, brother! Remember? I swear you're nuttier than a Christmas Fruit Cake! Haven't you figured that part out yet? Geez! Norman Bates ain't got nothing on your ass."

"Oh you self-righteous asshole! I'm not crazy! You're just jealous 'cause my dick is bigger than yours!

That's why Father Mereaux wanted me and not you! I've got a big dick! So ha!"

"Oh you idiot! I swear! Of course your dick is bigger! You killed me when I was eight years old, ya shitbird! I didn't get a chance to grow a dick thanks to you! All this drama you're causing is for what? *I* should be the one walking around this bitch angry, not you!"

Nico busted out laughing at the absurdity as he stood bleeding.

"That's prepost... preposter... That's crazy!"

"The word you're looking for is preposterous, and no it isn't. I'm fuckin' dead, Nico. And I *have been* for three damn decades. You've been talking to me all this time and I've been dead since we were children! You killed me. Killed your own brother just for the hell of it- just for the sake of seeing me take my last breath... In fact if I remember correctly, as I was laying there coughing up blood, you were laughing and dipping your fingers in it like it was finger paint!"

Nico rolled his eyes refusing to believe any of it.

"Yeah right! You'd say anything to get a rise out of me! You're so jealous that it's criminal."

"We're a modern day Cain and Able, you and me, but you seem to forget that part. Like I said, you've been a raging lunatic for decades."

Nico shook his head and dusted himself off.

"Oh really? And all this time I thought I was a Pisces."

"Very funny, jerk off," Lucien replied. "From where I'm standing, it looks to me like you're talking to a dead man. So I'd say that qualifies you for the funny farm."

Nico threw up his bloody hands.

"I'm not crazy, you dick, I'm a politician! And you're *not* dead! You're standing right there!"

"Trust me, Nico. I'm pretty dead. You pushed me down some stairs and I'm pretty sure I didn't make it."

Nico rolled his eyes.

"I wish you *were* dead sometimes. Maybe if you were, you wouldn't talk shit to me all the time. I'm the big brother you know, not you! I should be talking shit to you! Not the other way around. But oh no, it's *Nico you didn't do this or Nico you didn't do that.* Then I go and try to polish myself up and make myself presentable for the public and all you wanna do is make me think about *her*. I *hate her*! I hate that women whose stinking pussy birthed me! I hate every inch of her!"

Lucien leaned his head back and laughed as hard as he could. Nico felt the stinging of the cuts on his face and the pain in his side. His chest heaved with horror. He hated to think of *Maman* and what he'd done to her. He shook his head no, trying to get rid of the thoughts. It was too much. He fell to his knees and felt the tears swell in his eyes.

"But Lucien, why can't you understand? Can't you see I *had* to? She would have killed me. She beat me and beat me. Then she made me go to confession and that man did things to me. He touched me and made me *suck* him! And *Maman* let him! Right there in confession! Said it was my repentance. Don't you see? She would have killed me in the end."

"You mean the way you killed others," his brother replied.

"No! That's not it! That's- not- it! I didn't kill anyone! I don't kill, Lucien! I don't kill! You know that! They're all accidents!"

"Oh please, you're a gotdamn, cold-blooded, serial killer! What else would *you* call it? Take some responsibility, man! When you turned seventeen, whatever the hell is wrong with you really took over. You'd killed people- a lot of people, but when you turned seventeen, you killed your own mother. That's got to be the worse crime that a crazy fuck could commit! Face it brother, you're a vicious killer."

"NO! I AM *NOT* A KILLER! I'M A KIND HEARTED SOUL WHO SOMETIMES HAS

ACCIDENTS AND PEOPLE END UP DEAD!
THERE'S A FUCKING DIFFERENCE!"

"Oh, I see, that's what it is. You're right, no serial killer tendencies there at all," Lucien said sarcastically.

Nico beat the sides of his head and screamed from the depths of his belly. He closed his eyes so tight that he could see purple spots in the darkness. He moaned like a lost soul. He could smell the iron scent of coagulated blood all over the floor.

Father Mereaux sat tied to his chair with his head hanging limp on his shoulder. His small, red, penis with the hairy mole on the shaft, laid lifelessly on his thigh. His clerical collar was dyed red from all the blood that covered him, and slimy eye tissue hung from his eye sockets in disgusting, red, gushy clumps. Nico had picked the priest's eyeballs out with his fingernails.

He had taken great pleasure in doing it too. A priest with a red clerical collar wasn't a priest of God anymore anyway. No. He was a disciple of Satan, and in Nico's opinion, that suited the priest much better. Nothing about the priest should have been considered holy or godlike. God would have spit him out of heaven when he died, so he was only fit to meet The Devil anyway. And Nico was going to make sure that the priest met The Devil in the worst way possible.

Likewise, Maman was also tied up. She was on her knees in front of Father Mereaux's chair with her arms tied behind her back. So were her legs. Her huge, massive body sat motionless in front of Father Mereaux waiting... waiting for what was to come.

"Let me go," Maman said softly in that husky voice of hers, attempting to hold her composure.

She knew all too well that her demented son was going to make her suffer. He wanted to hear her scream. He wanted to condemn her to hell by making her watch the horrible things he'd done to Father Mereaux, but she wanted no part of it. She refused to look at the blinded priest who somehow clung to life.

To be quite honest, she was scared shitless of what her son would do to her. But God had chosen this role for her. God had chosen her to go through these tests and trials. There was no way that she would give Nico the satisfaction of seeing her scared. Fear was not an emotion of God. And a woman of God shouldn't show it to the face of the Devil. And that's exactly what Nico was to her as he stood towering over her.

"Tell me you love me, Maman. Tell me that you'll protect me from Father Mereaux and never hit me again!"

Maman shook her head.

"God will determine your fate, Nico. I will tell you nothing. You are a monster and you've been one since the day you split me open to come into this world. No one but the most Holy could ever love you."

"Tell me you love me woman or I swear to God I will cut out your fuckin' tongue!"

"Love is for the kind. It is for the deserving. You are neither. You are an evil incarnation of something that hell spit out! I could no more love you than I could love a pile of dog shit!"

In a blind rage, Nico kicked his mother in the back of the head, with a sickening crack! She fell over pitifully.

"Get up! Get up you, filfthy bitch!"

Nico kicked his mother in her sides trying to get her to get up. He wanted her to feel every ounce of pain that he'd experienced as a child. She was barely conscious. Blood poured from her mouth and her eyes were growing low and lethargic. Nico grabbed her by her short hair and forced her mouth open.

"You will do what Father Mereaux made me do! You'll open your mouth! Since you don't want to love me, you can love him!"

Nico punched his mother in the mouth, knocking several of her teeth out. Thick red blood poured from her lips and smeared all over her face. Maman whimpered and groaned in response with her eyes rolling in the back of her head. Nico, ignored the cuts on his knuckles and forced Maman's mouth onto Father Mereaux's limp penis. Her blood smeared all over the priest's thigh.

"Suck it!" Nico demanded. "Suck his hairy dick! Suck that mole that tickles him so good! God will forgive you if you tickle his hairy mole!"

Nico pushed his mother's head down onto Father Mereaux, filling her throat with the priest's lifeless penis. He pushed her head into his crotch over and over again, up and down, up and down.

"You like that, bitch! You like the way it tastes! Suck his little red weenie!"

Nico's chest heaved up and down as sweat beads formed on his brow. He could feel the tingling of sexual desire pulsate through him. He pulled out his own penis and began stroking himself in harsh static motions as he stared at Father Mereaux's pitiful meat jammed into his mother's throat. He moaned in ecstasy as he watched the blood from his mother's mouth leak all over Father Mereaux with foamy red bubbles collecting at the sides of her lips.

"Suck itttt!" he screamed weakly as he brought himself to climax. His juices squirted uncontrollably onto the side of his mother's face and ear as he fell to his knees. Maman's body sagged as she began to lose consciousness.

"You deserve this," Nico whispered as he shook with pleasure. "You deserve every inch of his dick rammed down your throat! You love dick! All cunts do!"

Lucien stood in silence watching the entire scene play out. Nico turned to face him and smiled, feeling pleased with himself.

"She deserves this. Aren't you pleased I finally got her back? I finally paid the old bitch back, Lucien! She deserved it!"

Lucien said nothing but shook his head no in horror.

"Yes, she does! She does too deserve it! Say it, Lucien! Tell her that she deserves it! You know just like I do!"

Nico turned back to the horrid scene of the blinded priest with his picked out eyeballs and his sexually violated mother. He stared at them feeling powerful, and that power filled him to the brim. It was like a high from a drug. It made him feel like an all-powerful god.

"My cup runneth over, Lucien! My cup runneth-"

Suddenly, something within him broke, and his high began to deflate like air out of a balloon. Overwhelming regret washed over him like sin, making him feel like he wasn't worthy of living. What had he just done? He blinked, trying to get the image to disappear, but it just wouldn't. It just wouldn't go away.

"Oh my God, help me Lucien," Nico pleaded as he wiped his eyes of sudden hysterical tears. "I- I just

wanted her to love me. That's all! It was love! Love made me do it! I love her!"

Lucien began to fade. Nico felt his stomach churning.

"Lucien, no! Don't leave me, please! I'm sorry! I didn't mean it! Please don't be angry! You're all I've got! It's love! This is all love! A little love never hurt anybody!"

Lucien faded completely, leaving Nico feeling deserted. He looked back at his mother.

"I can fix this, Maman! I know I can! I promise I can! I'm gonna make you proud! Watch!"

Nico rushed over to his mother happily and placed a white Magnolia blossom in her hair that he'd picked for her fresh just that morning.

"See that? Beautiful! Now you're beautiful, Maman! I made you beautiful, don't you see?"

Maman said nothing. Her eyes rolled into the back of her head so that only the whites were showing and her body began to seize and shake. She bit down on Father Mereaux's penis uncontrollably. In seconds, dark blood squirted everywhere and spewed from his lap. Maman had bitten his penis off right at the root.

Father Mereaaux screamed inhumanly, convulsing in sharp jerks. Mere seconds passed and he'd bled out so much that he fell over dead. Maman continued to shake and seize as the flaccid penis slid further down her throat, cutting off her air supply. She gasped for air frantically, unable to breathe.

Thick mucus from the back of her throat surrounded the penis and sealed her air passages completely.

"Grarrrr! Barrrrghhhh!" she vocalized horribly.

Finally, her body gave up all together. It gave one last violent jerk, and then was dead. The white Magnolia blossom fell from her hair and to the floor, coating itself with fresh blood. Maman's huge body hit the floor with a thunderous thud that shook the tiny shack.

Nico stared, horrified. His stomach curdled and churned as he watched his dead mother's huge body lay lifeless with the priest's bleeding penis still hanging out of her mouth. And where was Lucien? Why had he deserted him that way? Nico wailed with emotional pain as the room instantly filled with the smell of fecal matter streaming from his burning anus.

CHAPTER XVIII

Aleera rushed into the house as fast as her legs would carry her, hell bent on getting a few of Marielle's things so she could get the hell out of there for good. She had decided that Ole Marguerite was right. Staying there even another hour would have been crazy. So she figured maybe she'd just throw in a few dresses and purses and be out of there in 20 minutes. Certainly she'd be okay for 20 little minutes.

Now that she knew what she was up against, there was no way in hell she was staying there another night. She did feel a bit of love for Nico, so she would at least suggest that he come with her. After all, if he did, he would come with his money and that would put her in a beneficial situation. Besides, there was no telling what Marielle had in store for him so it was his best bet to leave too. But hey, if he didn't want to come, to hell with his ass. What good was it to have money or to marry somebody with money if you ended up a zombie and couldn't use it?

She ran up the stairs like a mad woman out of breath.

"Nico! Nico! Where are you? Nicoooo!"

She ran into their bedroom where she found him sitting on the floor butterball naked in front of the fire place. He was still wet, as if he had just gotten out of the shower, but he looked dazed and confused. There was glass all over the floor from a shattered mirror, and his face had tiny cuts all over it. Aleera rushed to him.

"Oh my God, Nico! We've got to get out of here! This place is possessed and Marielle is going to turn us into zombies!" she screamed frantically. "Grab your stuff and let's go!"

Nico looked at her with bewilderment clouding his eyes. He felt as if he had just relived his mother's death all over again and wasn't sure what he should do, let alone go anywhere.

"Huh? Zombies?" he asked slowly feeling dazed.

"Yeah zombies, muthafucker! That's what I said! That stuck up bitch you married is gonna turn us into zombies! Didn't you know what she was? *Bizango*! She's a part of *Bizango*! You idiot! You married her and she's part of a gotdamn secret society that makes zombies!"

Nico sucked his teeth and rolled his eyes not really in the mood to entertain stupidity. He'd just killed his mother for God's sake. "That's nonsense! Marielle is dead."

"No the fuck she's not!"

Nico could feel himself getting angry all over again. He pushed Aleera away from him, not wanting to hear anything against his wife especially when he was feeling so tender about his mother.

"Don't you say another word about her, do you hear me?" he snapped. "Don't you say one more word about my wife! She was beautiful. She was absolutely beautiful! And she's proud of me! She's proud of what I've become even if *Maman* isn't!"

Aleera could feel herself losing it. *What the fuck was wrong with everybody?* Even now she could feel the jealousy take over her emotions. She had been attacked in that house thanks to Marielle, and now Nico had the audacity to talk shit to her like Marielle was some kind of saint? *Hell to the nah!*

"You fuckin' weak ass bitch!" she screamed unable to control her word vomit. "After all this time, you're still in love with that hoe? She possessed you! She possessed this fuckin' house and made you punch me and you're still in love with her? You're so fuckin' weak! So fuckin' stupid! I should just let her turn you into a zombie! You deserve it! You would let her kill me before you'd believe me about what she's doing!"

Nico placed his hands over his ears to drown out Aleera's voice. He shook his head no from side to side like a child on a playground. Aleera rushed towards him and tried to pull his hands down.

"Listen to me, gotdamn it! Marielle is going to kill us! She's going to kill *me*! Don't you care?"

Nico's eyes changed instantly. He looked at Aleera feeling his heart surge with love and protection. All the anger faded away. Even the air seemed to change.

"I never told you how much I love you, Marielle," he said sweetly. "I never told you. You're just so beautiful. I'm sorry for what I did to you. But you have to see that I did it because I love you. I killed you because I needed you with me always. Don't be mad about it baby. I won't ever kill you again. I promise."

Aleera frowned. *What the hell was he talking about*? He grabbed her and brought her face close to his. She looked in his eyes and saw nothing of the real Nicodemus.

"Nico?" she asked feeling afraid.

"Mari, you were the perfect wife. You were the mother I never had. I didn't know it, but I needed you. I'm so sorry for the things I did, baby. I'll do anything you want me to. I just need you to love me. Tell me you love me, Marielle. Please."

"That's not Marielle, idiot!" Lucien said laughing.

Nico turned to face his brother feeling enraged again and let go of Aleera. It was time to get him straight once and for all.

"You're an asshole! I don't need you reminding me that I fucked up every day, Lucien! She needs to know that I love her! None of this would have happened if I'd just told her that I loved her!"

"Look at her, fool! *She's* some smutty slut you brought to live in Marielle's house! That's not Marielle! Marielle is dead! You killed her, remember?"

"I know she's dead! Do you think I'm stupid? She just needs to know that I love her! Now shut up and let me tell her!"

Aleera watched in horror as Nico carried on an argument with himself. He was different. His eyes were cold, but the black evil wasn't there. That creeping cold feeling that had come all those other times- that feeling that had shaken her down to her bones, it didn't come. This was the real Nico. This was the madness that dwelled within.

"Nico?" she called to him meekly.

"Your mistress is calling you," Lucien said tauntingly. "You might want to answer her."

"I don't have a fuckin' mistress, Lucien! Don't talk about mistresses in front of my wife! You think I'm trying to get a divorce? Marielle doesn't play that shit!"

Aleera gasped realizing that Nico had lost it. He was talking to himself. Making fun of himself and responding angrily like it was an argument between two people.

"Oh my God, Nico," she whispered frightened.

She ran out of the room and down the hall like a track star. At that point, it was fuck Nico. There was no saving him. The least she could do was save Marielle's clothes and get the hell out of there. Then she'd continue on with her life without all that crazy secret society bullshit.

CHAPTER XIX

She kicked open the doors in a hurry, telling herself that she'd only take a minute. She'd grabbed two duffel bags and bombarded her way through Marielle's closet, determined not to leave that house without something- anything. She snatched haute couture gowns and dresses off of hangers like a maniac, stuffing them into her bag. She grabbed a few purses and stuffed those in too. When she couldn't make it all fit, she jammed her foot in the bag, stomping everything in as quickly as possible. In the other bag, she emptied a couple of Marielle's shoe racks. There was no sense leaving those *Louboutins* in there as if someone was going to claim them.

"I'm gonna get something out of this shit. There's no way in hell I'm leaving with nothing," she muttered to herself as she tossed shoe after shoe into the bag.

Southern trees bear a strange fruit… blood on the leaves and blood at the root…

Aleera gasped. She looked all around the closet feeling fear grip her heart. There was nobody there, but she'd certainly heard somebody singing.

Black bodies swinging in the Southern breeze...

"Oh my God," she whimpered suddenly realizing that coming back for clothes was probably a bad idea. "Oh my God, please!"

She grabbed the duffel bags and tried to make a dash for the double doors of the closet, but they slammed shut immediately. Aleera screamed- her chest was heaving like she had asthma.

"No, please! I'm leaving! I don't want Nico! He's all yours! I'm leaving!"

Strange fruit hanging from the Poplar trees...

The soft, melodic voice faded to a whisper and the creeping cold that was associated with the fear and evil in the house never came. Aleera waited a few moments and heard nothing. She sighed and slid to the floor relieved. It was gone.

Aleera ran her fingers through her weave and reached on the inside of her fitted hoodie for her flask. She needed a drink- bad. As soon as she tipped the flask to her lips, she was suddenly pulled up into the air upside down by her leg! Before she could even get the chance to scream, she was violently thrown into the wall over and over again!

"Noooo!" she screamed as she was tossed like a rag doll repeatedly. "Noooo!"

She could feel laughter- evil laughter vibrating throughout her body as it slammed up against the wall.

"Let me goooo!" she screamed frantically.

Instantly, she was catapulted into a full length mirror in the closet, shattering it to a thousand pieces! Pieces of glass stuck in her arms and legs, and a few in her sides creating a bloody mess.

GET OUT, a demonic voice demanded. Aleera coughed and spit up foamy blood as she bled inwardly. She crawled to the doors of the closet and pushed it open, leaving the duffel bags of clothes.

"Now you've done it! Now you've really done it!" Nico exclaimed angrily to no one at all as he marched his way into the Swan Room after having thrown on a pair of sweat pants and a white tee. "Now you've pissed Marielle off and she's singing! I can hear her all over the gotdamn house! This is your fault!"

"There's nobody singing in here, moron! You're crazy as hell! It's all in your imagination!" Lucien exclaimed.

"I'm not crazy, I hear her! Tell him, Marielle! Tell him you're in here singing because he's pissed you off like the limp dick he is!"

Aleera cried out, afraid of what she was seeing. She did her best to crawl away from Nico and towards the door of the Swan Room. She didn't know what the hell was going on, but something was very wrong.

She inched along the floor to the doorway of the bedroom and managed to get the bag of brick dust out that Ole Marguerite had given her. She poured some down hoping that maybe somehow it could help save her. She knew that things were getting dire. She was beginning to get cold and that only happened when you were losing too much blood and dying.

She spread out the crumbled red brick at the doorway with trembling fingers while laying on her belly. She had to get it down before Nico got to her. Somehow she knew that if she didn't hurry, she'd be dead soon whether from the attack in the closet or an attack from her crazy ass boyfriend. Either way, shit was about to get ill.

Down the hall, a door slammed and Aleera felt jittery thinking The Evil was coming again to finish her off. She could hear rhythmic footsteps approaching. She looked back over to Nico and saw him sticking up two middle fingers at someone who wasn't really there. Suddenly it began to grow bitterly cold. *Oh God...*

She could hear the clackety click clack of heels on the wooden floor coming down the hall way. Her heart pounded in her chest.

"Who's there?" she called out in a quivering voice.

Charlize rounded the corner and stopped short of the brick dust in the doorway. She looked down at it then back at Aleera wonderingly.

"Visited a hoodoo woman?" she asked curiously. "Got yourself a little protection, did you? Or at least attempted to get yourself some... Not like this little puny mess you've made all over the floor is really going to do anything to help you."

Aleera watched Charlize linger in the doorway making sure not to touch the brick dust.

"You fuckin' bitch. I knew you had something to do with it! I knew you were the one trying to curse me! You! It was you all along! All this time I thought Marielle was haunting me... trying to turn me into a zombie from the grave! And all along, it was you!" she screamed, then fell into a fit of coughs, bringing up more blood.

Charlize laughed as she looked down at the crumbled brick and then back at Aleera.

"Oh please! Me turn you into a zombie? Why the hell would I want to do that?"

"I know all about the powder you plan to use on me, Charlize! Revenge for Marielle! For stealing her husband! You think I wouldn't find out what you were up to? All this time you wanted me to think Marielle was possessing Nico and this house when it was really you! But you can't hurt me!"

Charlize shook her head, letting the smile fade from her face.

"You look like you're hurt enough to be quite honest. And you're bleeding all over these nice wood floors making a dreadful mess."

Aleera wiped some of the blood from her mouth as she lay on the floor looking up at Charlize.

"You can't cross this brick dust line to use the zombie powder on me. Ole Marguerite told me that anybody who means me harm can't cross it. You've lost, Charlize! You can't hurt me. You can't use the powder on me."

"Zombie powder, eh? Some say there *is* such a thing... some say," she said seriously. "But I'll tell you what, *Madame*... It isn't *me* you should be worried about. The old hoodoo voodoo ladies tell you to put down this brick at the door and it protects you from those that mean you harm. You think you're saving yourself from me? Please. I have no reason to harm you. I don't like you, that's true, but making zombies and hurting others is a sin against the soul. You think I'm going to risk burning in the fiery pits of hell for you? I don't think so. No, you're sealing yourself in the room with the person who means you harm, sweetie. You're about to have a very shitty night. I almost find myself feeling sorry for you… almost."

Aleera looked back at Nico nervously who was still brandishing his fists at a person who wasn't really there. Something inside her told her that Charlize's words were true. Nico was the real threat. She felt it deep down where her biggest fears lived.

Suddenly it seemed entirely possible that Nico had lost his mind or maybe he'd never had it. The way he constantly mistook her for Marielle.... The way that he protected the Swan Room as if it were a shrine... The way she sometimes caught him talking to himself as if he were talking to a real person just as he was doing now... She had been living with a crazy man all along and it was all too clear that he was dangerous. He had come home on more than one occasion covered in blood. Her breath caught in her throat.

"*Mon dieu*[44], it's getting late. Well, I guess I'll leave you to *Mesieur* LaCroix," Charlize said matter of factly. "I'm sure you lovebirds want to be alone. Storm gonna get worse I hear, anyway, and I'd like to get back to my family tonight before things get too rough. *Bonne nuit*[45] , *Madame*."

"What? You can't leave me here," Aleera pleaded. "Not like this!"

---

[44] *Mon Dieu*- my God
[45] *Bonne nuit*- good night

"I do hope to see you in good health in the morning. And if I don't, I'm quite sure your soul will either be trapped in this house like mine, or you'll be a zombie. Either way, it's lights out, party's over, cakes on the griddle and you've already been greased," Charlize said chuckling to herself at her favorite *House Party* quote. She may have been stuck in the house for 200 years, but at least Marielle had gotten her cable to watch. She turned to leave.

"Wait! Wait, Charlize!" Aleera exclaimed. "Help me! What do you mean I'll be trapped in this house! Help me, please! I'm hurt! You can't leave me here to die!"

Charlize looked back. "It's much too late, *Madame*. You should have left while there was still time. Now, it's just too late. Try to take care as best you can. It doesn't hurt- maybe just a little pinch here or there. I promise. Just close your eyes and don't fight it."

"What?"

With that Charlize headed out of the Swan Room and down the grand staircase. Aleera whimpered pathetically as she tried to inch her way to the doorway. But almost instantly, she felt a hand grab her violently by the back of her neck, breaking the string that held the *gris-gris* bag that Ole Marguerite had given her. The little leather-like bag fell to the floor, spilling powder everywhere. *Damn it!*

Nico stood staring at her with his eyes looking blacker than she'd ever seen them. His face had somehow morphed into something evil just like in the movies when a person transforms into a demon during possession. His mouth curled unnaturally into a menacing snarl, baring white teeth that looked strangely dangerous.

"N- Nico?"

The air in the room grew so cold that Aleera could see her breath. She had never felt fear when looking at Nico, but now she feared for her life. It seemed so confusing! She didn't know who her real enemy was. Was it Marielle, Nico, Charlize, the house, The Evil... who? Maybe Nico hadn't been possessed just a few minutes before when he had been talking to himself, but he was for damn sure possessed by something now. .

"B-baby? Is that you," she moaned in pain.

The creature that was Nico cocked its head to the side at an impossible angle making the hairs on Aleera's neck stand on end.

"Nicodemus' soul is no longer his own! He belongs to *Bizango!* He will be punished for his crimes!"

Aleera squealed with terror as her blood turned to ice. Nico's voice dropped eerily in bass, but sounded like a chorus of evil voices all in one. His hands rested at his side, but Aleera saw that he held a metal free weight.

Where the hell did he get that? Her heart caught in her throat.

"Wh- What do you want?" she demanded swallowing a bit of the irony blood that had collected in her mouth. "Who *are* you?"

Nico let out a low growl like a rabid wolf.

"We want to hear you scream!" the chorus of voices replied in jagged unison. "And we are *Bizango*! We are many! And you-will-dieeee!

There was a sudden sharp crack, then a spray of dark blood against the wall. Aleera slumped down against the wall and slid to the floor. Her bottom jaw hung from her face as blood poured in thick streams down the front of her *PINK* hoodie. An iron scream bubbled through the blood sounding more like a death rattle as her body reacted to the horrific pain.

Aleera struggled to inch her way towards the doorway. Maybe if she could cross the brick dust, Nico would be trapped in the room.

The Nico monster approached her slowly holding the free weight raised above his head as she struggled to get away from him.

CRACK!

Aleera's head hit the floor with a sickening thud. This time the side of her skull caved in taking her right eye with it. Another blow whistled through the air bringing the free weight down against Aleera's head. Grey brain matter leaked out on the floor, and Aleera's body ceased to move. It was over. Just like that, she was dead.

CHAPTER XX

Nico stared at Aleera's mutilated, bashed in head. It was too much blood. Too much red, but something about it made him feel pleased. He stared at the carnage for a long time, smelling the metallic scent of her blood. He even dipped his hands down into it and tasted it on his fingers. It was salty and irony.

> *Southern trees bear a strange fruit... blood on the leaves and blood at the roots...*
>
> *Black bodies swinging in the Southern breeze*
>
> *Strange fruit hanging from the Poplar trees...*

Nico heard the singing which immediately brought him out of the strange fascination he seemed to have with Aleera's blood. When he finally looked at the mess he had made, his gut wrenched and churned. His eyes widened in strained horror as his mouth fell open and belted out the most piercing scream any human had ever heard.

"Oh my God! Aleera! Lee! Is that you? Get up! Get up! You can't be a Senator's wife like this! You have to get up!"

He fell to his knees, crying like a new born baby. He felt so helpless looking at her. He picked up a few of her skull fragments from the floor and tried to piece them back together like a puzzle, but the brain matter just wouldn't stop leaking. Instead it dripped like chunky mush to the floor in soft splats.

"Oh God, why? Why, Lee? Why? What happened! What happened here? Oh my God! What can I do! Speak to me, Lee!"

The dead splatter on the floor formally known as Aleera said nothing. There was just the constant drip dripping of blood from the caved in part of her head onto the floor. Nico sat beside her on the floor, holding his knees with his head down as he cried like a baby. It all washed over him in a nauseating wave and he could feel his stomach yearning to release a stinky pile of feces. He had wronged Aleera. He had wronged Marielle. He had wronged Lucien, *Maman*, and Father Mereaux as well. He'd wronged all those women he'd killed. He was just wrong. His existence was wrong.

"Don't cry, Nico. It's not so bad. You had to know it wouldn't work with her anyway," Lucien said soothingly.

Nico sniffed and shook his head yes.

"I know, but I really didn't mean to do it this time, Lucien. I didn't know it would end like this! I mean look at her! What the hell happened here?"

Lucien sighed.

"You know exactly what happened. You went ape shit again and killed the girl. That's what happened."

"No! No I didn't do this. No, I couldn't have done this. And if I did, it wasn't my fault. I didn't mean to hurt her."

"Nico, Nico, you Simple Simon. You always say that. You never mean to hurt the people you hurt."

"I really don't, Lucien. You know it. You know I could never hurt a fly. I'm as gentle as a peaceful lamb. Imagine me hurting someone," he chuckled. "The thought is ridiculous."

"I really think that Dr. Thibideaux released you from that psych ward way too soon after what you did to *Maman*. You were still at an impressionable age. My God, you were only seventeen. You needed just a bit more counseling. Just a bit more therapy on what to do if you ever got the urge for The Bad Thing again… I suppose it's really not your fault. You can't help that you feel those urges to do The Bad Thing."

Nico nodded. It was true and he was glad that his brother was being much more understanding instead of judging him the way he had earlier. Maybe Lucien was right. Maybe they *had* released him too soon. Twenty years hadn't been enough. He needed more. Maybe if he had had a few more years with Dr. Thibideaux learning those relaxation techniques, he would have been a better person. He wondered if he could go back? He was so tired of doing The Bad Thing and getting caught. He was tired of shitting himself when he got upset or emotional, too. All in all, he just wanted to be normal. Couldn't the world just forgive him?

"Does this mean I can't be Senator," he asked sadly in a small voice. He looked up at his brother with his big brown eyes and long curled eyelashes wet with tears. His perfect, kissable lips were poked out sadly like a child's.

"Of course it doesn't mean that. You can be anything you want to be if you stop doing The Bad Thing. Don't worry. I know you'll make us all proud someday, Nico. You'll see. Just like our great ancestor. You just have to pull yourself together."

Nico nodded feeling better. Maybe things would be alright after all.

"I know somebody who might be able to help you, but you can't go see her like this. You can't go in there talking like a little kid. She's really powerful and if you want her help, you'll have to be the Nicodemus LaCroix I know you can be!"

Nico looked up at his brother with renewed hope from the pep talk.

"Really? You know someone who can help me with all this mess?" he asked gesturing at the bloody carcass with the smashed in head lying on the floor. "But I thought you hated me, Lucien. Why are you gonna help me now when you hate me?"

"Marielle has asked me to help you, Nico. She speaks to me from this side. We're both dead ya know, we talk a bit."

"Now wait a minute! You haven't been hittin' on my wife have you, Lucien? You know she's mine! Dead or not, she's still mine and you better keep your filthy, dead hands off of her before I fuck you up!"

Lucien rolled his eyes.

"Shut up and listen before things really go to shit. I'm trying to help you here. Now, Marielle says this person can really help you. All you have to do is listen to her. She says she mentioned the woman to you once before- that the woman was a healer of sorts."

Nico beamed with joy as he wiped his face with bloodied hands, smearing Aleera's blood all over his face.

"Marielle wants you to help me? So she forgives me then? She forgives me for everything?"

"Uh... uh...Yeah sure, Nico. I reckon you're forgiven. Don't worry. Marielle told me everything. She says you need to go see *Madame* Sepion in the *Vieux Carré*[46]. She's some kind of famous voodoo woman out there. She helps people in need. She lives where the spirit world meets the living. Don't worry, you'll be able to feel it in your flesh when you've come to the right place. But you gotta go soon, Nico! *Bizango* don't like the things you've done and they want to give you a terrible punishment for what you did to Marielle. They want to turn you!"

Nico climbed to his feet covered in Aleera's blood and with brain tissue dripping like melted ice cream.

"They want to turn me into what?"

"You know what, Nico. You have to go now. You have to go now before it's too late. *Madame* Sepion can help you and keep you safe. She can help you turn your life around, but you have to go now!"

"Go now? What do you mean? Have you looked outside? It's raining cats and dogs!"

Lucien shook his head.

"Do you wanna die, fool? Get your ass out of here and go see *Madame* Sepion!"

---

[46] *Vieux Carré*- French Quarter

"But I don't know where my keys are!" Nico protested childishly. "Damn you, Lucien for making me rush! Where are my keys? You know I'm no good to anyone when I'm in a rush. And I can't possibly lock the doors without my keys. What if there's a burglar?"

"Try your pockets, genius," Lucien commented.

Suddenly Nico could hear faint laughter filling the room. Cruel laughter. *Her* laughter.

"You hear that," he asked Lucien. "You hear her? She's here! I know she's here. She's come home to me."

"Get your ass out of here and find *Madame* Sepion, Nico! You're crazy, remember? None of the shit you hear in your head is real. Not even me. Now get going before things take a turn for the worst."

"I'm not crazy, Lucien! Stop calling me names! You're really starting to hurt my feelings with that shit. You act like I've set some little orphans on fire or something. I'm not that damn deranged."

"That's debatable," Lucien replied.

Nico rolled his eyes.

"I swear I hear her. She's here. She wouldn't be here unless she forgave me for all that I did to her. Can't you see she loves me?"

Lucien shook his head and rubbed his hand down his face. "I can see this is going to be a long night, that's what I can see."

Nico ignored his brother.

"Come to me, my love. Let me tell you how much I love you. Let me tell you what I couldn't tell you before. I'm a changed man. I'm gonna be faithful to you this time."

All the doors and windows suddenly slammed open and closed over and over and over again! The covers on the bed pulled themselves back and the wing chairs flew into the walls. The huge portrait of Marielle shook and rattled as the face in the painting seemed to grow angry. Nico looked from left to right watching the show.

"That's new," he replied unfazed. "Maybe she's just as excited as I am."

"She's here to kill you, fool! Run! Get out! Find *Madame* Sepion!" Lucien screamed.

"But wait a minute, you just told me she forgave me. I'm confused."

"I lied. Get to *Madame* Sepion."

"Lucien, she's the one who told you to tell me to go to *Madame* Sepion. Of course she forgives me!"

"No she doesn't! She's going to cook and fillet your ass if you don't get out the house! Can't you see she means to kill you? What do you think all this is? A welcome home show?"

Just then a wing chair flew through the air and hit Nico square in the chest sending him flying. He slammed violently into the wall and fell over with a thump.

"Do you believe me now?" Lucien screamed. "Or do you think that was a love tap? Get your ass out of here before you find yourself taking a dirt nap!"

Nico climbed to his feet with difficulty.

"Mari, baby, I really think we should talk about this calmly and rationally."

In an instant, Nico slammed head first into the vase sitting on the marble coffee table. It shattered to bits and a piece of glass stuck in the side of his face, slicing it open. Blood spewed everywhere.

"Oh yeah, I can see what you mean, Nico. She's not pissed at all," Lucien exclaimed sarcastically rolling his eyes.

Nico groaned as he picked himself up again. This time he got the point. The curtains were whipping in an invisible wind, letting it be known that Marielle wasn't finished yet and the windows continued slamming open and closed. Nico limped as fast as he could out of the room bleeding from his face like a stuck pig. He certainly hadn't expected Marielle to be so angry. After all, he *had* apologized. What ever happened to good ole fashioned forgiveness? Especially when it was your husband you were forgiving…

He limped down the grand staircase, feeling The Evil breathing down his neck. It was like having the hot breath of 100 demons hunting you. It sure didn't feel like Marielle. Or maybe it was just a very, very infuriated Marielle. Either way, the feeling was sickening.

He ran out of the front door and down the steps of the porch into the pouring rain towards his black *Cadillac Escalade*. A red lightning bolt streaked across the sky, filling it with hateful light, then collided, with a harsh crack, into a tree right there in the yard. It instantly went up in flames.

Nico fell backwards, finally frightened, as the tree landed with a huge crash on his truck, caving the middle of it. Urine flowed freely down his pant legs as he pissed himself in fear.

"She means business," Lucien commented.

"Oh God, Marielle, please! Don't tell me *Maman* got to you too!"

EPILOGUE

`"That's it! That's the whole damn story! After that, I came here! And I'm sure you can tell that I really didn't do all that much wrong. I'm really a good guy. I just get a little riled up sometimes. So will you help me?" he begged as he held his stomach. It was beginning to feel a little bubbly. "I'm sorry about everything I did. I- I just wanted to be a Senator! I didn't mean to hurt anybody! Honest I didn't!"

Nico could feel his stomach boiling and bubbling. He squinched his toes together in his shoes hoping his anus would hold it all in. The last thing he needed was for his emotional bowel movements to release in the old woman's shack all over the floor.

The withered old woman stared at Nico with her blanched eyes. She wore an amused toothless grin on her face.

"Yeh be a evil man, *Meseiur* LaCroix. De spirits right 'bout yeh. Yeh doan deserve t' live!"

Madame Sepion tossed her head back and cackled like a banshee as the thunder rolled.

"Spirits goan' take you to hell an' back!"

"But wait a minute! I said I was sorry didn't I? I'm gonna make up all the bad I did with good. I'm going to be Senator and then everything will be okay!"

"*Kochon estipid*[47]!" the old woman cackled.

Nico's heart thundered in his chest as he swallowed. He suddenly felt very hot and sweaty sitting in the little shack with the old woman, telling the story of his sad life. He wiped a bit of the blood- Aleera's blood, from his brow hoping that he'd wake up tomorrow and it would all be a dream.

"Hahahahaha! Ain' no dream, *Meseiur* LaCroix! Ev'ryt'ing you done be real! An' ev'ryt'ing goan' happen be real!"

"What's going to happen? What are you saying? Are you going to help me? My brother said you would!"

"Yer brudda be dead! Worm food in de grave! An' so be you! *San Pwel... Bizango* got a lil somet'ing fer yeh, *Mesieur*. Yeh mess wit' de wrong *famille* when yeh mess wit' de Blanchards! Dey goan myake yeh pay!"

With a swipe of her bony hand with long yellowed nail, Nico felt a force send him flying into the walls

---

[47] *Kochon estipid*- Stupid pig in Kreyol

knocking the eerily lit oil lamp over. They were plunged
into total darkness. Nico could feel the yellowed nails
digging into the skin of his face, peeling it back, etching a
bloody cross into his forehead. He screamed and thrashed.

"Arggggh!"

Nico rolled over and climbed wearily to his feet as
blood from his forehead dripped into his eyes. Breathing
heavily, he rummaged through his pocket and found a
lighter. He lit it with trembling hands hoping for at least a
visual to get to the door before he shit all over the floor.
The feeble light gave enough luminance to show that the
old woman was gone. She was no longer sitting in her old
rickety chair. He gasped.

"Oh, Nicoooo!" a voice called in a sing-song,
playful way. "Over here, darling."

Nico turned to look behind him, and was suddenly
blasted in the face with a hot, yellow powder. The powder
seared into the cross on his forehead, burning him so badly
that his whole body began to sweat like rotten pig meat set
on fire.

"Gggghhhh! Mmmmhhhhhgggghhhh!" he
screeched.

Suddenly his body became stiff as a board. His
limbs wouldn't move at all. His mouth stopped moving
and his muscles became tensed. He fell to the floor like a
stone statue- his eyes wide open with fear and staring

blankly ahead. He could still see and hear everything, but he just couldn't command his body to move.

She stepped from the shadows, beautiful as ever. Black curls cascaded down her back. And she wore the blossom- the white magnolia blossom tucked into those beautiful curls. Her eyes flashed with green and brown as she stared at him with playful eyes. He'd forgotten just how beautiful they were, and the corners of her full mouth turned upwards in a victorious smile.

"Aww, my love... *tout bagay anfom*[48]?" she asked sweetly.

Nico couldn't say a word. His eyes were wide with the woman who stood before him- the beautiful woman who had been his wife for over a decade. The beautiful woman that he thought he'd sent to her death.

"You're a dead man, Nicodemus LaCroix. And now your soul belongs to me. As ye sow, so shall ye reap."

Marielle blew her husband a kiss and then smiled at *Madame* Sepion giving her a wink, who had seemingly magically reappeared behind Nico.

"Thanks for everything, *granmére*. You taught me well. Nobody wrongs a Blanchard and keeps his soul."

She turned back to Nico.

---

[48] *Tout bagay anfom*- Is everything okay in Creole (Kreyol)

"Byen veni pou esklavaj[49]*, Nicodemus."*

F   I   N   I   S

---

[49] *Byen veni pou esklavaj-* Welcome to Slavery in Creole (Kreyol)